HARBINGERS

JONATHAN CREED
BOOK 3

JOHN A. CURLEY

ROUGH
EDGES
PRESS

Harbingers
Paperback Edition
Copyright © 2023 John A. Curley

Rough Edges Press
An Imprint of Wolfpack Publishing
9850 S. Maryland Parkway, Suite A-5 #323
Las Vegas, Nevada 89183

roughedgespress.com

Paperback ISBN 978-1-68549-247-2
eBook ISBN 978-1-68549-246-5
LCCN 2023930271

DEDICATION

I have been very successful in my career because of one specific talent I have. I am able to find the best possible people to work with. All I need is to let them do their job, and I look good. Sadly, I have seen such pain that I never lack for inspiration. I have given up expecting that I will have seen the worst the world has to offer. Happily, when it comes to characters, the heroic ones I do not lack for inspiration.

I would like to thank my partner, Ron, on whom the character of Ray Gordon is based. Ron grew up in a difficult situation and left home to join the Navy at the first opportunity. He spent 15 of his 20 years in the US Navy as a SEAL. What makes the SEALs the most elite Special Forces Units in the world is not just their ability to make someone meet their maker from 1,000 yards away, but that they all possess exceptional intelligence. He is by anyone's definition of the word a hero—although he does not consider himself so. He once walked away from five million dollars in funding from an investor who had approached me. The investor offered funding directly to Ron with the intent to cut me out. As he rose from the table to leave, he responded to the investor, "I am here to support John, not to steal from him." He can also rattle off physics formulas in such a way Richard Feynman would be impressed.

I would also like to thank my partner, Mike, on

whom the character of Chief Mariano is based. The Chief is exactly as I have written. From the moment you meet him, he is impressive, and readers are sure to become more impressed with him over time. He carries an imposing collection of injuries, having been shot, stabbed, and stomped on. There is a superb article in *New York Magazine* that was written about him entitled "Captain Midnight." It is worth the read. I was with him once when we saw a car accident where a woman jumped out of her car, trying to get to her baby in the back seat. Mike checked out the baby—who was fine—reassured the mother, and even comforted the distraught young man who had accidentally hit the family of two. As he was calling the precinct and telling them to send a car, the woman asked me, "Who is that man?" I told her his name and that he was a Chief in the NYPD. She looked at me—surprised—and said, "He's a Chief? And he stopped to help us?" That's when I realized that most people wouldn't stop for a fender bender on their day off.

I asked Mike about that later, and he responded, "Well, John, that's what I want my cops to do, what I expect them to do. How can I not do the same?" If you don't think leading by example is outside the norm these days, I'd have to disagree. It's rare—except in my circles.

I would like to thank my other partner, Jeff. I have known him since 1988, and we have been through many a hair-raising incident. He treats me like a son and has looked out for me since the day I met him. He is the quintessential investigator. Although he has told me from day one that a good investigator always has a pen. There is not enough space to detail how impressive his career has been, so we still rely on his judgement and experience.

I want to also mention George Smith and Anthony Dasaro, both of whom taught me not just martial arts but helped prepare me for life. If I have good things inside of me, they exist largely due to these men. Smitty raised his son—on whom a character is based—to be a compassionate man. Now, he's a gifted physician who risked his life at ground zero and in Haiti after the earthquake. I am privileged he is my friend.

Thank you Vivian Potter. A super class act, an incredibly smart and tough cop with a heart of gold who's hotter than the surface of the sun all rolled up into one. She didn't just kick cancer's ass—she sent it running, and her feats of bravery could be a book all on their own.

Steve Orlando makes a brief appearance, but he's a guy that knows the meaning of what family is. You'll see more of him in the future.

Carl, Dwayne, Clarence, and J.T., although gifted with considerable brawn, were often the reasons—along with the previously mentioned Valkyrie—why running security at nightclubs was a cake walk.

Tom Manfre, whom I have learned a lot from and who is always a good man. Johnny Cool Rico—aka Jeffrey Lawrence Greico—is even cooler than his character. But not quite as cool as he thinks he is.

Clint and Terry are guest characters in this book, and you will come to know them in the next series I'm working on. A walking natural disaster and a sewing machine knife guy who sent the grim reaper packing. Both of them have rescued children and punished those who have hurt them.

Bernie Kerik and Tony Shaffer are also briefly mentioned. Thanks goes to them. Tony gave up his military career for this country, and I will never forget that when those towers came down, Bernie stood up.

Speaking of heroic people, thank you to one of the coolest couples there is—two of my most favorite people, Clint and Queen Jahn. They are cooler than they appear, authors, warriors and transcenders. They, like so many, share the loss we will never get over. Thank you for your help, guys.

Thank you to Lisa Davis for her input.

I often see people, especially younger people who lack role models as well as direction. When I was young —which is both yesterday and forever ago simultaneously—part of my direction came from reading. Robert B Parker's Spenser, Mickey Spillane's Hammer, as well as less obvious characters like Stephen King's Ben Mears and Tolkien's Aragorn were some of my heroes. With my father gone, and after reading of people like that, I gravitated toward real life counterparts, just a few of whom I have mentioned in the preceding paragraphs. It is one of the reasons I consider myself so fortunate to be with Wolfpack's Rough Edges Press.

If you are a parent reading this book, I hope you consider having your children—if they are old enough —read not just my books but other books from authors you'll find at Wolfpack like Mickey Spillane, Wayne D. Dundee, and my dear friend, Andrew Vachss. Just to name a few.

We need people like that. We need them because— if you haven't realized it yet—while there are good people in the world like my characters, there are evil ones as well. No law, no political ideology, and no amount of wishing can deal with them. The only counter for evil, violent people are good people also skilled in violence.

Keep that seat at the bar open for me, Papa Vachss. Remember the deal, pal. To quote you after our first conversation, we will speak again.

HARBINGERS

EPIGRAPH

"The meeting of two personalities is like the contact of two chemical substances: if there is any reaction, both are transformed."
— Carl Gustav Jung

"Being deeply loved by someone gives you strength while loving someone deeply gives you courage."
— Lao Tzu

"I believe that many people who were abused as children do themselves and the entire struggle a disservice when they refer to themselves as "survivors." A long time ago, I found myself in the middle of a war zone. I was not killed. Hence, I "survived." That was happanstance, just plain luck, not due to any greatness of character or heroism on my part. But what about those raised in a POW camp called "childhood?" Some of those children not only lived through it, not only refused to imitate the oppressor—evil is a decision, not a destiny—but actually maintained sufficient empathy to care about the protection of other children once they themselves

became adults and were "out of danger." To me, such people are our greatest heroes. They represent the hope of our species, living proof that there is nothing bio-genetic about child abuse. I call them transcenders, because "surviving" (i.e., not dying from) child abuse is not the significant thing. It is when chance becomes choice that people distinguish themselves. Two little children are abused. Neither dies. One grows up and becomes a child abuser. One "passes it on." One "breaks the cycle." Should we call them both by the same name? Not in my book. And not in my books, either."

— Andrew Vachss

PROLOGUE

WHEN I WAS UPSTATE, outside of Washingtonville, I was eight minutes away from the Dungeon. What I call the "home" I "grew up" in. I had told myself there was no need for me to go there. Yet I ended up there.

It was falling apart. It had never been sold. It was almost a certainty that it was referred to as a haunted house. And it was. I was just intending to pass by, but I found myself in the front yard. The front door was open about six inches. The interior was dark, and when I pushed the door open the grey light of an overcast, fall day reluctantly shone in. It made the room brighter, but it was almost like the light didn't want to be there. Or felt it didn't belong in that place. It was fall after the foliage had dropped and winter was reminding you it was not far away. It was cold, bitterly so. I wouldn't go in the building. I wouldn't call it a house or a home. I told myself I wouldn't go in, but, of course, I found myself inside anyway. There were signs of use. Kids from the area probably went there and hung out. There were couches that looked like they had been thrown away and dragged in. It even looked like the fireplace had been used recently.

The iron bars of my makeshift prison were still there. Efficiency was one of the monster's traits. Economizing the available space, the monster made my cell under the stairs by removing the cosmetic paneling and putting up iron bars. I lived in that cell for the first eight years of my life, under those stairs. The filthy mattress —if you want to call it that—I used to sleep on was still there. A bowl also, I'd been given water in. I felt hot and began to sweat. I was afraid but also angry. Very angry.

There was a huge hole in the middle of the ceiling, and it lined up with another hole that, had there been illumination, you could have seen through into the second floor and its ceiling. I wasn't curious even though I had never seen the second floor. When they used to film the freaks raping me, if one of them complained that I smelled bad, they bathed me in a dog tub in the basement. The water was always ice cold. Although once, it was hot enough to scald me, punishment for failing to move quickly enough. I stared at the center of the living room where the monster had died. An inch of dead leaves lay on the floor, scattered beer bottles and cans. There was one torn up converse sneaker. I knew it wasn't mine; they had never given me shoes or sneakers, and it had to have been left there after the investigation had been completed. There were holes in the walls, and I could hear now and again the sounds of small animals scurrying around behind them. Surprisingly, most of the windows were intact, and it would be fairly warm if the door was closed. There was that smell of rot, and I could see water stains on the sheetrock. All the paint was gone.

As I stared at the middle of the living room floor, I remembered the cop picking me up and taking me out. Walter Hertman was his name. We still stayed in touch to this day, probably the only two people left who exchanged actual letters through the mail. I stared at the spot on the floor where the monster's body had lain after Walt had shot it. As I stared and remembered, the thing that called itself my father began to materialize, there on the floor. On the front of its shirt, a dark red circle began to expand where Walt had put three rounds from his .357 only inches apart, center mass. The huge knife the monster had raised above his head was now on the floor next to him. His eyes glassed were over.

I remember staring even as Walt covered my eyes and hugged me. I told him "My dog," and I reached for Rex. He was a puppy the monster had killed the night before. It strangled my pet while I watched. As I stood there, a tear rolled down my face on the left side. The monster had left Rex's body for me to play with, laughing about it with his friends. He told me if I was good, if I behaved myself when they made the video, and if I did as I was told, he'd bring Rex back. You see, I had not come to him right away when one of his freak friends showed up with his freak wife, the night before. He had gotten the video equipment out and was setting it up joking and laughing with the two freaks that had shown up. Others had arrived earlier in the day. I knew what they were going to do to me. I knew how much it hurt, and I hid under the blankets holding Rex. Pretending not to hear them and making believe I was sleeping. That's why the monster killed my dog.

As I turned to leave, the monster stood there, before

me, smiling. I knew I'd see it when I turned. I was not afraid. I wasn't surprised. Somehow I just knew. He was smaller than me now, and I weighed fifty or sixty pounds of solid muscle more than him. I didn't shrink, I didn't cower. It was the opposite. I felt the muscles in my chest and shoulders ripple and bunch up. I clenched my fists. I flexed and loosened the muscles in my body and felt the strength and power that I had built up for years. Every time I picked up weights, punched a bag, ran up hill, sparred, and all the times I fought in the bars I worked, I built my suit of armor—armor between him and me. Each workout made it thicker. Every time I went onto the mat, into a ring, fought in alley, I made my armor stronger. I would never be hurt by the monsters again. I was no child now.

"Happy to see Daddy?" I heard the monster ask. Its lips didn't move. I heard it in my head. But that was its voice, just as I remembered and still heard in my nightmares.

I spat in his direction. When I spoke to it, I pronounced each word and took my time so the meaning would be understood. "You were many things, none of them good. But you were never my father. I am the Adam of your labours, but I am not what you wanted me to be. Fuck. You," I said this as I walked through it and toward the door.

"You are mine. You are his. You are his servant."

I stopped, but I didn't turn around. "I am happy you're dead. Although sometimes I almost wish you were alive, so I could kill you myself. It's a shame you didn't suffer more."

PART I

HAM

PART I

HAM

1

I WALKED THE SECOND FLOOR, watching with Carl and Dwayne in tow. "The Way I Are" blew through the speakers. An artist formerly known by some other name had shown up unannounced and was apparently a big deal. Without any warning, his "security" had walked him into the middle of the dance floor. It was Club Music night. Dance music from the 70s through today would play. Some nights we had bands, big acts, and some nights, new bands from a record label we had a contract with. On some occasions there were private parties, movie premieres. We were, at this point in time according to everyone in the know, the place to be. I still carried ear plugs on Hip Hop Night. That was the only night we had to use metal detectors. If gravity knives, brass knuckles, and illegal firearms could be given as Christmas gifts (and that would suit some of my friends just fine), I'd be set after those nights. We didn't voluntarily have Hip Hop Night. Someone wanting to rent the venue would send in a middle aged college professor type, rent it, pay for it, and we'd find out when they advertised it. The contract had changed so that we could refund their money and deny them, but it was up to the owners. I didn't care for the music, but music is subjective. The violence that came with it, plus the music, well that was another story.

The crowd, upon realizing a celebrity was in their midst, broke over him like a big wave on a small beach. My guys pulled him out and one of them got banged up a little. We escorted him to a booth. Clarence and Joe guarded the only two ways to get to the booth. Joe was big, about 6'2" and close to three hundred pounds. To say Clarence was big would be like calling Everest a hill. He stood almost seven feet and well over 400 pounds, yet somehow he had no waist. When you took into account how fast and strong he was and how smart he was—and that was key—I often thought that the mythos of various different Gods would have been based on people like him. The black skin of his face was expressionless and ageless. Dwayne and Carl moved apart as I stopped, and we scanned the crowd from the railing. The second floor was like one large circular balcony, and you could see the dance floor better than if you were on the first floor in the crowd.

Foster, the manager, had hired me six months ago. It took me almost ten days to get the crew assembled. They had been open two years. They'd just become "The Night Spot," and they'd had four lawsuits in the six months before I got there. The song finished, and The Gap Band dropped their bomb. As I scanned the crowd my eyes rested on her. Damn, she was here again. I stared. I had no idea who she was, yet she'd kept me company every night since I had been a kid. I paused on that word, as it went through my mind. Since I was a kid. My hand started to move toward my forearm, where the burn scar was. Well, I promised myself tonight would be the night I talked to her, if she came. There were always plenty of women, but it was starting to occur to me sex was good. Love might be great. And rare. It took me seeing her three times before I realized she was the woman I went to bed with every night since I was old enough to remember.

I was thirty-five when I first saw her in person, and it had to be a sign. Love had happened only once, and it wasn't mutual. But now... Hell, I hadn't even talked to her yet. She was laughing and talking to one of the girls in her group. She was tall, at least my height. Light olive complexion, long black hair, and beautiful warm brown eyes. Jesus Christ, I didn't even know her name and I'd go through a brick wall to get to her. I was already thinking the honeymoon would be in Aruba or Hawaii. Her eyes rested on me, and as she looked at me she smiled. I smiled back, something I rarely did at work.

She was wearing a kind of black dress and light make up, but her black hair, as opposed to being up and out like most of the girls had, was long and fell naturally past her shoulders. Her breasts were exactly the right size. She was athletic, not thin, and she curved in all the right places. She was Italian or maybe Greek. I swear to God I had never seen a more beautiful woman in person my life, and I had seen most of the popular movie stars and models. There had to be something to her. I didn't have a specific type. Most women are beautiful in one way or another. I'd heard her talk and watched her. I just knew she had a heart. Was I influenced by how beautiful she was? Maybe. But it turned out I was right.

I worked up the courage and was about to go and talk to her, when "Jungle Love" came on. I gritted my teeth and grimaced. I wasn't fucking talking to her with that song on. I looked over the crowd. They liked the song. Foster made his way to me.

"How do we look?"

"Except for the incident of that idiot being walked into the crowd, quiet." The music blared louder. "Relatively speaking," I nearly shouted.

He smiled. "You caused quite the stir. I told them I'd admonish you, and that you were upset about a man getting hurt. I suggested he call you or have his manager call you to upgrade his security."

"Appreciate that," I said. "Not much chance of that now, would be my guess."

After we pulled this blessing to society up from the floor and saved his ass, we got him to a table. His "security" made their way to the table. As I gave Joe and Clarence their instructions, the guy who was the in charge of security for the star formerly known as something else grabbed my arm. I figured he was the boss because while he was on the ground trying to get up and getting kicked in the head, he looked the most important. He smiled, and I was prepared to say "no problem, but next time let us know ahead of time you are coming." He wasn't thanking me, he was warning me.

"I just want you to know, you and your guys...you can't ask him for his autograph." As he said it the currently nameless star nodded gravely at me.

Clarence had heard and looked down expressionless. I took a deep breath and started to turn away, then said fuck it. "Let me tell you what, asshole," I told the head of amateur hour as his big deal of a boss looked on and continued nodding to emphasize he couldn't interact with the peasants protecting him.

"You fucking clowns walked him into the middle of the crowd, he got swamped. The guard at Macy's knows not to do that. We saved your asses, his included, and instead of thanking me you're warning me? One of my guys is in the back after getting hurt saving you morons. Let me tell you what," I said in a low but angry voice as the music was not playing at the moment. "The only place I'd want his autograph is on a fucking check. Fuck you and fuck him."

Apparently the star wasn't used to that and looked horrified. The security guy's jaw dropped and my guys chuckled. Clarence's normally impassive face showed the hint of a smile.

"Well, officially I'm admonishing you. Personally, you were too nice to him. Assholes." Foster saw me looking at the new focus of my existence.

"You have good taste, Ham."

"I'd argue if I could, Boss," I said. He laughed.

I liked Foster. He was the manager. The owner had an arms manufacturing plant in Germany. Foster drove a Bentley. He didn't need to work, but he liked to. As a result of the aforementioned spate of lawsuits, The Club's insurance company had dropped them. There hadn't been another lawsuit in two years since I had been there. When I had asked him where he was from, because he spoke absolutely flawless English, all he'd said was Europe. On one of the rare nights we had a problem, he was in the thick of it. I saw him move and was happy he was on my side. He had the bearing military guys often had. I knew how to use my hands, but my primary asset for the job was my brain. It was simple: they gave me leave to run the security how I saw fit and paid top prices. I wasn't greedy, though. I paid the best men what they were worth, and I kept the peace. We hosted events where people paid a couple of grand to get in—you don't manhandle people like that if you want your club to stay on top. I kept the peace. Long before "Roadhouse" came out, I realized the only way to make real money in club security was getting paid for the guys. We worked four nights a week average. Anywhere from 12 to 15 guys (a few females in that group). I paid them twenty-five bucks a night better than most clubs paid their doormen, and I pocketed 60 bucks a head plus the $185 for me if I worked, and I usually did. Since running security at "The Supper Club," which rarely served dinner, I had picked up two more clubs and a bunch of side work, including a heavy protection job I had zero qualifications for. But I knew a retired Secret Service agent. He handled it and we spilt the proceeds. I'd made 50k from that job, securing an estate in The Hamptons. We were getting a similar job, and Barry, the ex-agent, and I had agreed he'd staff it and I made him a partner.

Dwayne and Carl would be leaving soon. If we got the two new clubs I had gone to that week, which would make a total of five, with the two I had before I got here, things would be jumping. I might not be able to be in two places at once, but they were the next best thing, actually better. The only thing that really stopped the business from growing faster was the guys. There were plenty of big guys around, but that alone didn't come close to cutting it. They were both about my height, 5'10". They were both well over 300 pounds, and my 240 pounds disappeared behind them so you couldn't see me. Dwayne had a record for squatting in one of the powerlifting organizations—over a thousand pounds. Carl benched close to 700 and he did the strongman contests. Both of them had to have genius level IQs. Dwayne was a Captain in the FDNY and doubled as my fire safety guy, and Carl had a trucking business. They were both coming into the business as well, and I gave myself an easy out and told them they had to come up with their replacements and help me hire their staff. I had asked Clarence first because he had seniority, but he wanted to wait until he retired. He was a teacher and he also ran the NYC Lifeguard Guard Program for the Parks Department.

HANDS DOWN, I had the best crew there was. Having guys that were good with their hands but had restraint and were a visual deterrent was the key. And we trained two or three times a month together. Smitty, a guy I knew in Staten Island, had a dojo and we'd meet there every other Sunday of the month and work on tactics. Once a month was voluntary, but just about everyone made them when we had them. Those that did would get pay raises and stayed on the primary list. J. T. Tyson, another of my top guys, ran the NYC Corrections SWAT team at Rikers. He had just brought me a bunch of new guys from his job looking for off hours employment.

Athena, as I referred to her in my head because I couldn't call her Sappho, was still looking at me. When I saw that I smiled again. I signaled a cocktail waitress and asked her to buy Athena and her friends a round on me. Foster nodded his head. The very first time I saw her in the club was not the first time I had seen her. I had seen her every night I had gone to sleep since I was old enough to notice her. First in the Dungeon, and then after the Grants adopted me. First, they fostered me and then eventually they adopted me. Adoption. I shook my head at the thought. They damned near bankrupted themselves making it official. I couldn't understand, and actually asked them about that when I got older. No one was going to adopt me. I was eight. I'd need therapy. I could see it on the faces of the people that worked for the city while I stayed at a facility, and when they came to visit me at the Grants. Odds are I would not turn out well. If I didn't go bad after what happened the whole first eight years of my life, I'd have a lot of issues. But the Grants, the only people I'd ever call my mother and father, loved me. No one was going to adopt me. They would have had it a lot cheaper if they just fostered me. It shouldn't be called an adoption. It should be called a benevolence. I shook myself out of that line of thought. I had work to do.

My full name, Hamilton Sebastian Grant, which had been responsible, ultimately, for more than one school suspension, wasn't utilized by many. The waitress went to Athena, and her smile, which I believed I would do almost anything to see, broadened. She motioned her friends over and they all waved at me. I gave a slight bow.

"Connected" by Stereo MCs came on. A few minutes later when a tray of drinks arrived the girls all raised their glasses to me, and I waved. As "Butterfly" by Crazy Town came on, I motioned for Carl and Dwayne and they came over. They leaned in and I asked them to keep an eye on things as I'd be taking a break for 15. Now or never.

I walked towards her. My hands were starting to shake. She was looking at the dance floor and her friend saw me and whispered to her. She turned and saw me and smiled again. Jesus Christ that smile would melt the Arctic Circle. She walked towards me, and before I said anything, she leaned in and kissed me on the cheek. Not to sound corny, but that sent a shiver down my spine. A good one.

"Thank you so much for the drinks, that was very considerate," she said. "I'm Sophia."

"Everybody calls me Ham," I said. "I have a fifteen-minute break. Would you have another drink with me?"

"Love to," she said. Corny as it looked, I offered her my arm and she took it and we walked to the small private bar on the second floor. Vinny, the guy I had posted there, opened the small gate. I ordered a Manhattan with Southern Comfort on the rocks. She ordered Vodka and grapefruit juice.

"What is Ham short for?" she asked me.

"Hamilton," I replied. "My mother was apparently hoping I would get into a lot of fights," I said with a grin. I called Eileen my mother and not my adopted mother. She had been my mother. She was the only woman I would ever refer to as such. I could never tell her when she would ask me what was wrong, almost every night for the first few months I stayed with them, that I was waiting to see if she or Noah hurt me.

"It's a nice name," she replied, laughing.

"Listen to me, dear lady," I said, looking at her. "You shouldn't lie to your future husband."

She burst out laughing. I smiled wider. "That is a

novel line," she said. "Most guys would be afraid to make a joke like that."

"Well, who knows? If we do get married, you can tell the kids that I told you that five minutes after meeting you." And it would turn out years later, she would in fact tell our kids just that.

She lived in Staten Island, and as I did also, that was perfect. She worked as a waitress and bartender. She smelled wonderful. We talked for 15 minutes, and I knew I had to walk the club soon.

"Would you please have dinner with me?" I asked her.

"I would love to."

I apologized to her for needing to work, and she told me that it was okay and that she was so happy we talked. As I went to go I placed my hand gently on the side of her beautiful face. I leaned in and gently kissed her lips. No tongue, and I kept the distance between us and didn't press against her. She kissed me back, softly. You'd have to know me to understand how unusual this was. I was shy for the most part. Not that I hadn't been with women. I'd been doing club work since high school. I met women all the time. Talking to them...was hard. Relationships, real ones, were harder.

It was hard for me to get close to women. Nothing much helped. Years of therapy didn't do much of anything. Nightmares were still a nightly thing. I'd thought about having some of the scars removed. I'd even talked to my friend Ken, a gifted cosmetic surgeon, about removing them. But I never followed through. A few tattoos covered a couple of them. I had a tattoo of a broken heart on my chest with my sister Christine's name under it. The people I refused to call my parents killed her when she was six.

I am always respectful of women. Actually, I try to be respectful to everyone. I had never kissed a woman just after meeting her. I don't know why I did except that it felt right and I wanted to...very much. We broke the kiss and looked into each other's eyes. Her beauty was overwhelming. It was tangible, and it was all of her.

I had paid a couple of hundred bucks for a course about picking up women. That didn't help. I found that being cold and distant, according to them, especially in the beginning, made me seem like a mystery. The women I was unsuccessful with were the ones I tried to get to know and open the door and let them know me. So, learning I was naturally attractive to women because I was distant was what the 200 bucks I paid got me. Then apparently when the time came to tell them all about me, which was later on, I didn't and then I lost them.

"You are so beautiful, I don't think I could accurately describe you, Sophia. You made my night." The radiance of her smile would have made the sun look dim. She gently placed her hand on my cheek now, and I pressed her hand against my face, briefly, then left the balcony. I was hoping my heart rate would slow. If you knew me, shy was an understatement.

I had been upstairs about 20 minutes, and I motioned to Dwayne and Carl and we went downstairs. The three of us were working together tonight because we were looking for someone in particular that might be in the crowd. One of the waitresses had an ex that was threatening to violate a restraining order. She was a sweet kid, and she just had a kid, his kid. She had come into work with a bad black eye, and Foster got out of her what happened. He was apparently accusing her of sleeping with Foster or myself. Neither was true to my knowledge. I liked her. She worked hard to support her kid because that piece of garbage didn't work. She was renting a room from my cousin who, like me, had been on the school weightlifting team and we had been personally trained by a guy named Bill Hinbern. The boyfriend wasn't stupid and wouldn't make an appearance there.

A sweep yielded nothing. The Artist formerly known as something looked away when I spoke to Clarence and Joe. I had 15 guys on that night, and Vivian. She watched the ladies' rooms and was the second gun. She'd stay after while the receipts were counted along with a guy named Tom Manfre. He was retired PD and one of the nicest guys I've met. Despite him having a very bad shoulder injury, last time there was trouble I turned and found him at my side. Vinny's voice came over the radio.

"Ham, private bar second floor. The kettle is on."

"Copy that, on the way. Clint, Terry, meet me there." Back up I went, letting Carl and Dwayne work the main floor.

Clint Overland and Terry Trahan were in New York for the next eight months. They had a job they worked during the day at a building in Brooklyn and had been recommended to me by a PI I knew on the Island. Clint ran 6'5" and was 300 pounds of rock solid muscle. In his youth he had been what we would call a bad guy, and later on God and the love of a good woman changed him. Which was fortunate for the rest of us. A walking natural disaster would be an accurate description of him if he was angry. He now, among other things, was a preacher and he made a real effort to try to keep young men from walking down the path that he had.

Terry was about an inch taller than me and I had 50 pounds on him. I saw a video of him where he was teaching some form of martial arts that incorporated knife work. He moved like a fucking sewing machine. I'd seen him use his hands and he was just as good without the knife. He was John Doe. He walked the crowd with a colored drink in his hand and he blended in. One of the reasons we rarely had trouble was him. He had a talent for reading situations, and if there was going to be trouble he'd know. A Flock of Seagulls came on and sadly I couldn't run away.

We all arrived there at the same time. There were two lawyers apparently. Drunk and preparing to engage in a hair pulling contest. The problem was the group of guys with the taller lawyer. We knew they were lawyers because the private bar area of the second floor was rented by a law firm for their employees. Apparently one of them brought guests. The shoving match and the potential hair pulling had been quelled. Vinny had noticed the crew with the taller lawyer who I bet practiced criminal law. They were hard guys and out of place. We didn't do pat downs or metal detectors on nights like this, and I doubted these guys would have made it in if we had done either.

The guy to the right of the tall lawyer had a leather jacket on and I noticed his pants hung lower on the right side. I was betting gun. And I was further betting he did not have a corresponding permit. Terry had made it there first, and people took him for a patron. He had moved behind the thug with the low hanging right pant leg, as I had come to think of him. He was directly behind the tall lawyer and his two friends were on either side of him. And now Terry was behind him.

The organizer of the party, a young woman who worked for the firm, had come over and was apologizing for the incident. I told her it wasn't her fault and it was just a case of too much drink. The short lawyer, whose friends were likely other lawyers and were trying to talk him down, and the thug and his two friends slid in closer. Clint had eyes on them and Vinny did as well. Tommy Manfre appeared at my left shoulder again. The short lawyer started to calm down, apologized, and started to walk away. The thug whispered into the tall lawyer's ear. The tall lawyer began pushing forward and cursing. I moved the short lawyer to his friends and told them to take him in the back, and put myself in the tall lawyer's way. He put his hand on my chest to push me and I grabbed him. The thug reached into his jacket on the right side. Terry moved, Clint scooped up the friend on the thug's right, Vinny got the guy on the left, and the thug was on the ground. I caught the tall lawyer with the edge of my hand on his carotid artery where the vagus nerve was. He collapsed.

Tommy's gun was out. "Terry, did you see his waist?"

"Got it, Tommy," Terry said, coming up with a Browning 9mm. He ejected the round from the chamber, dropped the magazine and put that in his pocket as well. He moved so fast I didn't see what he did, but the thug wasn't going to be moving for a bit. Vinny pulled a knife off his capture and Clint found a carpet razor. Nice guys. Lauren, the girl from the firm who had hired out the Balcony, was horrified. I took her by the arm and walked her away from the crowd. At that point I saw

Sophia had come up and was behind me, holding a beer bottle. She had been drinking Vodka and grapefruit juice. Another indication it was love and not lust, I thought. I smiled at her and she blew me a kiss and went back to her friends. Damn, what a woman.

"Okay, Lauren, who is who?"

She looked at me quizzically. "Of the two parties who are they to you? Who is the shorter guy that was walking away and who is the taller guy whose friends have the illegal weapons?"

"Oh," she said, now understanding. "The attorney that was walking away is with our firm. He does patents. The one on the ground with the friends is the boyfriend of a paralegal we have. He practices criminal law in Brooklyn."

I nodded.

"He was being rude to a few people, and Maury, the patent attorney, asked him to lighten up. He was using some real foul language around the girls and he was making them uncomfortable. Robbie, the one you, um, subdued, started pushing him and attacking him. I just learned his girlfriend that works at our firm had broken up with him and he shouldn't have been here."

"Any input as to what I do with them?"

She shook her head. "I'm worried that the firm looks bad."

"Okay, I'll keep it low key," I said.

Two more of my guys had appeared and I walked over and looked down. The thug was stirring.

"Clint, would you do me a favor and please take their wallets and IDs if they have them and bring them all into my office. Tommy will go with you. If they are any trouble," I started.

"They won't be boss," Clint said. I smiled. There were few certainties in life. Clint was one of them.

"Thank you," I said. He looked down at me and smiled, and put his hand on my shoulder.

A few minutes later we were all in my office. The thugs were not looking happy. Their lawyer and would be co-combatant was less happy and was threatening to sue. Tommy had taken the IDs and called the precinct. The thug with the nine was out on bail. And he was represented by the attorney. They sat in the chairs, the thugs and their lawyer across from me. I stared at the lawyer who was still a little drunk. He ran his mouth until he locked eyes with me. He kind of trailed off and I remained silent.

"Ok. So, counselor, you show up at this party with a client who is carrying an illegal piece, which you likely knew about, when he is on bail which you likely got for him. You know how the disciplinary people are. You could be looking at arrest and disbarment, and this moron here is looking at revoked bail and sitting in Rikers until he pleas out to the current and new charges. From this point forward, shut the fuck up," I said to the lawyer. His mouth had hung open a while, and when his dulled senses let him know he was about to start drooling, he closed his mouth.

We were all quiet for a bit. One of the thugs looked back and forth from guy to guy, and my people either looked straight ahead or made eye contact with him. The air conditioner was on despite it being a little cool out because it was always hot in my office.

"As for you," I said to the lead thug whom we had disarmed. "What happens to you is first dependent on the gun. If it's a clean piece you have a shot of getting out of this. No worse for wear. If it's not clean, you're done."

"It's clean," he said. "I just picked it up. There are people I have to worry about," he said.

"At this moment you only have me to worry about. The gun goes to the cops. If they find it's been used in something they will be by for you. I'll be holding onto your driver's license until I know it's clean.

"Now get the fuck out," I told all of them. I called Midtown North and asked for Eddie Blake. We had gotten to be good friends, and things like this had happened before. It would go just like I said. If the gun was clean, I found it in the men's room. If not, he'd see to it someone picked up the thug and his friends. We had been introduced by Foster and Hans, the club's owner. It turned out we helped each other a few times. I had actually gotten them info on some people with warrants that liked to go clubbing. I had also stopped almost all the violence in every club I had. I spoke with Eddie and he told me he'd have someone come by for the piece and they'd check it out ASAP. My guys had taken the morons and they'd be escorted out. I rubbed my eyes and put my head on the desk. I didn't remember the last time I had slept more than a few hours. I thought about coffee, and the door opened after a cursory knock. Vivian came in.

"You look tired," she told me.

"Yeah."

"Insomnia again?"

"Of course."

"Ham, there's a very attractive woman outside. She said she's a friend of yours and you asked her to stop in before she left? Sophia?"

"She's good, let her in."

Sophia came in and Viv closed the door on her way out. Donna Summer floated in the room before Viv closed the door and I thought "Hot Stuff" was the right song for her, although a bit crude. She had almost no makeup on and she was beauty incarnate to me. She'd walked right out of a painting. I smiled and she smiled back.

"Would you like to sit?" I asked her as I stood. "Coffee, another drink? Anything?"

She shook her head and smiled. "I am the designated driver tonight," she said. "The only two drinks I had were the one you sent over and the one we had at the bar. I just wanted to make sure I left you my information. Your people are very impressive the way you guys handled that situation," she said.

"Thank you," I said. "They make me look good and they make my job easy. I did notice your participation, by the way. Thank you."

She smiled. "You're kind of cute and I wanted to make sure you'd be able to make our date." She handed me her name, address, and cell and home phone numbers. I smiled and grabbed a piece of paper off a pad on my desk and did the same, giving her my Staten Island office and home address (no, this was not usual) and my cell. "I don't have a home number, just the cell. Always the best way to reach me," I said.

"I've seen you, how you see everything that goes on, and how when something happens you are always in the middle of things."

I smiled. "Where is your car parked?"

"In the lot across the street," she said.

"Okay if I walk you guys over?" I asked.

"I'd like that."

"How would tomorrow be for dinner?" I asked her.

"Tomorrow would be great," she said, smiling and it was even brighter than before.

"I have the feeling we have a lot to talk about," I said. "How about we start with an early dinner? Say I pick you up at 5pm?"

"I'll be waiting," she said.

I went with her and called Carl over the radio and told him I'd be walking some people out and asked him to take care of things. It was near midnight. I was tired but happier than I had been in a while. She had three friends with her. Although none of them held a candle to her they were all pretty. It only took a few minutes to get them across the street, and the attendants knew me.

"Hey Boss Man," Efram, the head attendant greeted me. I slapped the high five he left out for me and handed him a fifty. He pocketed it and smiled.

"Efram, this is my friend Sophia and her friends. Please take good care of them when you can," I said. "Consider them staff." The girls all said goodbye to me and were genuinely kind. The awkwardness of me not knowing what to do since I had spontaneously kissed her earlier was alleviated by her kissing me the same way. I pulled her in close and held her briefly. She held me back. We looked at each other. I kissed her again, firmly but softly. She pressed up against me, and knowing it was way too early and that it would be crude for me to use my tongue, I took her lower lip between my teeth, very gently, kissed her again, as I held her face with my right hand.

"Wow!" she said.

"Look, um, I don't usually," I started. "I'm not

usually this forward. I don't know what came over me..." I was blathering.

"It's okay," she said. It's like she knew it was hard for me. "I'm so happy you did. I came here again tonight hoping to see you."

Okay, now I was sure that she could hear my heart beating and that I might be on the way to some kind of coronary overload. Did she just say that? I didn't know what to say. I looked at her and for the rest of my life I would remember exactly how she looked at that moment.

"I wish it was tomorrow," I said.

She laughed. "It is!" Sure enough my watch told me it was two minutes after midnight. "I'll see you in seventeen hours."

The crowd thinned out rapidly. The guy we were keeping an eye out for never came by and the waitress would get a ride home with Tommy Manfre and Carl. I saw Foster, he was okay made arrangements with Dwayne to cover for me tomorrow (actually tonight) and I left. Tommy and Vivian would secure the place, the bank down the block had a night depository and we had a procedure for making sure the money got there and my people were safe. I drove home. It only took me 25 minutes. Down the West Side Highway, through the Battery Tunnel, Over the VZ and home. I got in and Andy was waiting for me. I let her out in the yard. I wasn't hungry but I was, for a change, tired. Still I couldn't stop thinking about Sophia.

2

I SLEPT A SOLID FIVE HOURS. That was rare. I let Andy out and she tended her business while I made black coffee. It had finished going through the coffee machine as I let Andy in and she sat patiently and waited.

Andy, short for Andromeda, and yes when you're surreptitiously named after Noah's son, you gave your dogs names like Andromeda, watched expectantly as I took out two Milk Bones.

"Sleep!" I called out to her and she sat. I had grown up reading the Burke novels by Andrew Vachss and I can tell you from him being my law guardian, he was exactly who he appeared to be. Burke had Pansy. I had Andy. My parents allowed me to have dogs and we had cats, too. As soon as I moved into my own place I'd found Andy at a shelter. She was a pit, and a big one at well over a hundred pounds. She was a working dog. I slept soundly because she was there.

I put both bones on the floor in front of her.

"Sit!" I barked and she tore into the bones.

My dog wouldn't eat unless given a command. No one was going to poison her. I'd spent weeks training her myself. If I told her to protect someone she would do so like they were me. She ate her bones then came over to me. It was still pretty early. I'd gotten in a little past two and slept until seven-thirty. I felt my stomach rumble, but I never ate before I worked out. I drank black coffee and swallowed an Excedrin, an Advil, and a Primatene tablet. I had developed the habit from the weightlifting team at school. Andy settled, I set the alarm then headed to the gym. It was a five minute walk from the house and the walk served as part of the warm up.

When I was in high school and college I'd been a wrestler and weightlifter. I was good at both but I hadn't done them for the competition. I had done them for strength and to better be able to take care of myself. I had been into Judo and boxing. The last few years I had been studying Aikido. I wasn't able to go to classes often which I regretted. The man I found that taught grew up in Washington Heights. In most cases Aikido was not practical as a self-defense method. Melvin, however, was a different story. He changed things a bit. A wrist lock would be a wrist break. With my wrestling background I had been able to do well in the sparring, but he showed me really fast you wouldn't be grappling with a broken wrist. The locks and breaks helped a lot with my work and real self-defense in that order.

On the way out I stopped and looked at the painting I had in the living room. It was a hand painted reproduction of "Sappho" by Mengin. I had very little knowledge of art but I knew about this painting. I had two of the reproductions in the house and one in the office. I was thinking about getting one for my office at the club. Until I was eight, I grew up in what a lot of people would consider a concentration camp. The prior owner had left the furnishings when the creature that was my biological father bought the house. That sack of pus in human skin would never have bought the painting. I looked at the burn scar on my arm and shook myself out of the dark place. I had been cold one night. The thing that I would never call my father held my arm against an open flame when I told him I was cold and asked for a blanket.

The gym was crowded with hard cores. I did a brief warm up and started working the clean and press. I had raised some eyebrows in school. I was cleaning close to four hundred at the two twenty-five weight class, which they called the 109 kg class.

If I had devoted myself to it full time I might have made the Olympic team. I hadn't been training the lifts since early childhood though. I did use some juice early on but I wasn't willing to do the stuff that was required that would cut my life expectancy. I could still clean over 400 on a good day. I didn't see it as worth the time for the future it would give me. I was a little less than twenty pounds off the top guys in the states, which put me about 40 pounds behind the best guys in the world. If I had been willing to do the heavy stuff and devote my life to it, who knows?

It was a great sport and I enjoyed it, but there was little future with a 400 pound clean on your curriculum vitae. Now I lifted two or three times a week. I did sets of two or three reps and four or five exercises a workout.

I'd added some of the power movements and always worked my neck, forearms, etc. I'd run the other days and work a hybrid martial arts workout after the running days. I rarely missed workouts. I had started training with the Captains of Crush when they first came out. They were heavy steel hand grips. Carl and I both had closed the number 3 which took two hundred and eighty pounds of pressure to close. Although neither of us bothered with the certification we were two of around three hundred people that have managed to do that. But he could also close it with his left, I still had a significant gap when I tried to do it. Carl had almost closed the 3.5 he was close. I spent a good deal of time working my grip and hand strength.

I also went to the shooting range every month. We did money drops at the clubs so I had a carry permit. I often thought that if there was a hell, it would be eternally dealing with the NYPD licensing division.

I kept it light. In truth all I could think about was seeing Sophia and how not to screw it up. Which almost certainly meant I was going to screw it up. I was already thinking about how I'd deal with it if she didn't like me. Yeah, that's how I think. When I didn't care it didn't matter. There were always plenty of opportunities. Still, even though I'd barely talked to her, I felt like she might understand me. God, she was beautiful. I shook my head knowing there was nothing about me that warranted her being with me but I hoped still.

I left the gym, went to McDonalds, and ordered two breakfast sandwiches and scrambled eggs for Andy. I'm not much of a cook. I thought of Sophia again. Jesus, was I some kind of stalker? How weird was I? I was planning a future with her if she didn't reject me like she probably would, because she looked like what a painter imagined an early Greek bi sexual poet looked like, while she was on a cliff where legend says she was thinking about killing herself, which was almost certainly untrue. I knew, as a child, she would save me. One day the lady in the painting would save me from the monsters. The monsters in this case were real. And they were my "Family."

I picked Sophia up at ten to five. With my face burning red, I parked, got out of my car, and knocked on the door of the address she had given me. About thirty seconds went by and I was sure she wasn't home or she'd had second thoughts. I should have left the damned flowers in the car. I could hear music coming from the house. My heart sank. I had in just a few seconds, imagined her not being there or cancelling.

I knocked on the door again and this time I heard a woman's voice call out she'd be right there. I took a deep breath.

She opened the door and stood there, and I just about melted. She had on a white top and a brilliant smile. I almost cried, that's how beautiful she was. It was close to unbearable. She looked at the flowers and smiled even wider, even more brilliantly.

"I love flowers!"

I didn't say anything. It pretty much was going to end up that if she rejected me I'd drive my car into a wall.

"Come in," she said opening the door wide. "I just let Harley, my dog, into the back yard. Do you mind dogs?"

"Hell no, dear lady. I can't wait to meet her."

I don't remember much of what we said, I remember playing with Harley, her huge Rottweiler. He and I got along great. She laughed when I got on the floor and rolled around with him.

We went to Basilio's. It was a family owned Italian Restaurant on Father Capodanno Blvd, near the Verrazano Bridge. They had a garden in back of the restaurant and grew their own vegetables. We drove there in my car and we held hands as we did. She told me about her family and her life and I was fascinated by her. She had not gone to college, but she was very bright and started working when she was fourteen in a restaurant her family owned. She owned her house outright, no mortgage.

She asked me a few questions about me and my family which I avoided. She noticed me avoiding it and I rolled the dice.

"Listen, can I be forward?"

"Absolutely," she replied.

"I am having a great time with you. I do want to talk about myself and answer your questions but I need to ask you something first, and please be honest and I'll explain."

She smiled. "Okay," she said gently.

"When we are done would you like to go back to my place or your place for a drink? It's not a ploy for me to get in your pants here, I'm asking because I'd like you to finish telling me about you and I will tell you about me then."

"Yes, I'd like you to come back to my house and have some wine with me."

I took a deep breath and my eyes cast down. I looked

up at her and was again moved by the sheer undeniable beauty of her face.

She saw something might be wrong and put her hand on my arm and smiled. "Don't be so sure I don't want you to make some kind of play," she said in a very low and very sultry voice. I laughed.

"Okay."

We talked more about her and her family. She obviously loved her family very much. Her brother was a little crazy but she was very close to him and her two sisters. She had another brother that had passed away when he was young. She was still sad about that.

I remember little of the drive back to her house. It was early, not even eight yet. We walked arm in arm back to her house and she opened the door. In a little while Harley had been fed and curled up on a huge dog bed in the living room. She got a bottle of wine and two glasses and put them on her marble coffee table. We sat on her couch, and had taken our shoes off and she kind of intertwined her legs with mine as we sat.

She poured one glass of wine. She only filled it up about a third of the way. She took a sip and made sure it tasted good.

"Would you like to try some?" she asked me.

"Sure."

She took another sip, moved close to me, and looked at me...no, she looked into me. Her eyes felt like they were merging us. As I watched she drank more wine. She slipped in closer to me and put her lips on mine and let the wine go from her mouth into mine. Surprised at first, I can honestly say no one had ever served me wine that way. I tasted the wine and then her tongue and pulled her closer and held her as tightly as I could and kissed her deeply. She moaned softly as I kissed her and that nearly drove me wild.

I kissed her neck and the fragrance of her skin was maddening. If there were any signs she wanted me that much I didn't pick them up. Maybe it was because I was so worried I'd screw things up; whatever the reason, I hadn't picked up on it and now I felt the overwhelming need for her. I gently took off her top and slid her pants off and she unbuttoned my shirt. A few seconds later our clothes were in a heap on the floor. Passion overwhelmed any fear I had. I learned every inch of her body and held onto her when she'd climax and her body shook. It wasn't the awkward kind of sex people sometimes had the first time. I pushed her back on the couch and I pulled her on top of me and I was inside her and fought the urge I had to let go and kept everything slow and steady between us. She gasped and buried her face in my shoulder. I held her tightly as she shook. We didn't move and we stayed in that position after she climaxed.

"Where is your bed?" I asked softly.

"Upstairs, to the left," she whispered. I gently moved her off me and picked her up in my arms and carried her upstairs. We were together for hours. What I remember most was, it wasn't like our first time. It felt like we already knew each other.

There was a faintly illuminated alarm clock on the dresser in her bedroom. It read 11:45. She lay with her head on my chest and her arms around me. We both drifted in and out of sleep for a while.

"You want to sleep?" she asked me.

"No, I'm awake. You?"

"I'm awake, too. Can I get you anything, water? Anything?"

"Yeah, baby, water."

She got up and she was comfortable with me, herself, or both. I admired her form as she left the bed. She was only gone a few minutes and she came back with two water bottles and out clothes. She gave me a water, put hers on the night table and took my clothes and neatly laid them out on a chair. She took the t-shirt I had been wearing under my shirt and slipped that over her head and smiled at me. I have no idea why but that made me feel very happy.

"Can we talk a bit?" I asked her.

She smiled and nodded her head. I didn't have to do this. It had been a great night. It felt like the best night of my life. I could actually make love to her again and not talk, I wanted her again. This had never really worked out well before. No.

"Relationships are hard for me, mainly because I don't talk about things when I should and I don't share things that I should. I know this is probably not the thing to do and I'll end up scaring you off, but I have such strong feelings for you..." I trailed off.

She looked at me again. She inhaled and spoke very softly. "It's okay, talk to me." When I didn't say anything she spoke again. "Sweetheart, I feel strongly about you, too. I like sex as much as anyone but I'm particular about who I take to my home. I don't usually sleep with someone on the first date. And you just made love to me. It was like we've been together a while and you knew me. It wasn't just sex. And that, by the way, usually would send a guy running for cover."

I looked at her and was going to stupidly ask, "Are

you sure?" and like she read my mind she nodded and again, very softly she said, "You can talk to me."

I got up and put my shorts on; it just seemed to be the thing to do. You didn't talk about this stuff while you were naked. I took a deep breath.

"In the past I haven't done well with relationships. My family, if you want to call the freaks that raised me that, hurt me. The thing people would call my father made kiddie porn and he used me and my sister as what he called "actors." Until he killed her."

Her mouth opened and her eyes went wide. She was stunned; that was how people on the rare occasions I spoke of this usually acted. I cleared my throat.

"It isn't going to be easy and you need to know about this, so you can decide if you want to see me," I said gently. "Let me get it all out and I promise I will answer any questions you have."

She nodded. I brushed the tears off her face and I continued. "They were also what you would call devil worshippers. They had kidnapped other kids. We pretty much spent most of our time in cages. No one knew we existed. We never went to school. One of the people that my so called "father" bought drugs from and gave films to got caught and he ratted my father out. There was a big thing on the news when he got caught years ago. The headlines read things like "House of Horrors." It was on the news for months. This was in the seventies so there was no internet but you can find all kinds of articles about it now. I also don't call them, meaning my biological parents, mother or father. I usually call them what they were. Monsters."

I had been sitting on the edge of the bed but I got up

and went to the window. I could see the full moon through the blinds.

"My brother, though, was treated better. My father would say he was his heir, his first born. He actually killed my sister, as the monster gave him direction. She was always sick. She had fallen into what I know now would be a coma, due to malnutrition or a head injury or maybe a dozen other things. Or maybe all of it together. The monster showed him what to do. He was only a few years older than me. When I think back I'm surprised he had my brother shoot her to make sure she was dead. I'm surprised he didn't just bury her alive. It took me a long time to figure out it was a learning opportunity for his heir."

I stared at the moon a while. "My father made films of us, I can't really talk about that. He sold them to other freaks. He'd beat us if he felt we needed to be disciplined. And for most of the day we'd be left in cages or empty rooms unless it was to come out use the bathroom. He would say we were Satan's children. That we existed to be of service to the father.

"I remember when the cops broke in. They shot him when he charged them with a knife. The other monster, my biological "mother," they arrested. She died in prison a few years ago. I was in a hospital for a long time. I had an attorney, a Law Guardian. He came to see me at the hospital and then was with me during some court proceedings. He had some pull so he had me placed with this family he knew on Staten Island. My family. My Mom and Dad. Eventually they adopted me. I still talk to him every once in a while and I read his books. He's a writer also."

I felt her hand on my shoulder and I turned to face

her. She was weeping. She tried to say something and couldn't and just hugged me. I held her tightly. For a long time. I took her hand and led her back to the bed and we sat on the edge of the mattress. I looked in her eyes and though I saw she wept for the pain I carried, there was strength in her. Anger. She reached out and traced the heart on my chest.

"Here's the part you really have to know about. There was a painting in the building I "grew up" in. I'll never call that my home. It was a beautiful woman at the edge of a cliff holding a lyre. It's called "Sappho" by an artist named Charles August Mengin. He painted it in 1877. It's now in the Manchester Art Gallery in England. There are prints and copies made of it and there was one in the home. The creature that imprisoned me didn't have any appreciation for things like that. It was there when he bought the house and he never got around to removing it. I used to imagine the lady in the painting was coming to save me. When my real parents took me home I kept talking about it and we looked in art books and I found it. They asked me if I wanted a copy for the home and I said yes. They asked if I wanted them to get a print of it for *our* home. My real home. That is the only home I've ever had. They are my real mother and father. I have two copies of the painting. One in my home and one in my office."

I went to the chair where she put my clothes. In my pants was my cell phone. I took it out and unlocked it and went to the gallery of pictures I had. I pulled up the picture I carried with me. I sat next to her. She looked at me, her eyes still wet with tears.

"You look like her," I said. "This is actual love at first sight just because you looked like her. I never pray,

Sophia. But I prayed after I saw you, I prayed that you were exactly the kind of person you are. That your heart was just as beautiful as you were. I know you aren't the woman in the picture and that just because you looked like her that didn't mean you'd be a good person, that you weren't married, or that you'd even like me. I just had to try. And I won't blame you if this is all too much for you and if you don't want to see me again. I had to tell you these things because I...well, it still affects me. I have nightmares sometimes. I tend to become very pessimistic at times. It affects me in a hundred different ways and I needed you to know now. In the past when I haven't told women I was with they would just think I was cold and distant. And mistrusting. A few times I told someone about it and that scared them off. I couldn't not tell you and maybe have you come over and see the painting."

She reached over and got a tissue from the night-stand. She looked at me still, crying still. I held her hand. She looked at the picture of the painting on the phone.

"I do look like her," she whispered softly. "Oh, sweet-heart, I'm so sorry," she said. "I am so sorry."

I shook my head. "You don't ever have to be sorry for this, it's not your fault. They did it and I am okay now. Did I do right? Should I have waited? I want you to know if it's too much it's okay. I wouldn't be angry."

"No, you did right. I'm glad you told me."

I brushed the tears away from her eyes. "You are the most beautiful woman I have ever seen. You are also, in just this short time we are together, very kind and caring and I just felt that about you when I was near you. Don't feel this obligates you. I don't want that, either. If you're willing to see where it leads, I am, too."

"I do want to see where this goes," she said. It wasn't long before we got engaged. We also made a brief journey into hell together and now years later, as I write this, I cannot imagine my life without her. I know I don't deserve her, but I couldn't live without her.

3

"I HAVE this feeling now and again that this isn't going to work out, that everything will be ripped away from me," I told Carl while we were having coffee at the Club.

"Ham, for Christ's sake, you are happier than you've ever been. In a few months you are going to marry a woman you fell in love with because she looks like a painting you have. And she has a heart of gold, she loves you. After everything that happened to you in your life, maybe it is your turn to be happy."

The club was doing well. Foster was in demand, and although he exclusively handled the club, he started a management company and I had referred him to a few of the places I did security at. It was just shy of three months after my first date with Sophia and we were talking about moving in together. I had actually been out to see a friend, Lou Maddaloni in Suffolk County, about an engagement ring. I had told no one about that. We fell into place and I and just about everyone that knew us said we were the best thing to ever happen to each other. Yesterday I brought Andy over to meet Harley and they got along great.

I made it so Andy trusted Sophia and would take commands from her. Foster came in and asked for coffee and the bartender moved off to get it. He sat on my left side, Carl was on my right. We were doing a meeting tonight and all the management people were going to be there. Carl and Dwayne each handled a club. Tom Manfre and Vivian also came in and Sat at the bar. As they sat they all said hi and everyone in turn would ask me how Sophia was. I smiled. I was happy my work family had taken her in so quickly.

"Speak of the devil or angel in this case," I said as Sophia came in at the same time Clarence, Clint, and Terry did. Clint and Terry were technically off but came by for the meeting and because their wives had flown in from Texas for the weekend. I had reserved a special table for them and the ladies would be coming from their hotel in midtown in a little while. Sophia had actually just stopped by on her way home from visiting a friend. I was leaving after the meeting and had the weekend off and was going to be spending it with her.

Sophia kissed me and Carl gave her his seat and grabbed another one. We sat and talked and I got to watch Sophia, her face beaming the way it did when she was happy, talk with my people. She whispered to me that the guys in the lot across the street were holding her car. JT showed up and said hi to everyone.

I reflected about how happy I was and even as I did that I still felt that dread I always did, that I didn't deserve this and something bad was going to happen. After my real mother and father adopted me, for about five months the only trouble they had with me was that

I kept falling asleep at school. The teachers mentioned this but knowing what had happened to me they all chalked it up to the nightmares. But that wasn't it. After I had gone to live with them and after I came to understand they wouldn't hurt me I would wake up around 2am in the morning. I'd take this big butcher knife out of the kitchen and watch from the window of the empty spare room, on the second floor. They found out when I fell asleep one night and they saw the knife next to me on the floor in the spare room. I remember my mother crying when I told my father why.

"I have to protect you guys," I told them. "In case the monsters come." I remember my mother turning away crying, so that I wouldn't see her.

Sophia saw the change that had come over me and she knew and she leaned in and kissed my cheek. Foster had noticed as well and he leaned in and whispered to me "Be happy, mate, it's your time and you deserve it. Take happiness when it comes it's never guaranteed to stay."

The meeting was at ten and it was nine forty-five. Sophia told me she was going to go and would meet me around midnight. I grabbed Sean, a referral from a security job that Clint and Terry worked, and asked him to please walk Sophia to her car. She kissed me and left and everyone said goodbye.

I started going over in my head what we had to talk about, all good, and how quickly I could get it done and head back to see my woman—and then the gates to hell opened.

Five minutes later I saw Sophia hurrying back up the stairs with a very worried look on her face. She called my name and everyone heard it and stopped. I knew something was wrong and jumped off the stool and met her half way.

"Ham, something bad is happening across the street." She was breathing heavy, and not from running up the stairs. As calm under pressure as she was beautiful, she kept her voice steady as I listened.

"Sean was walking me to my car, and an old, beat up car pulled up. A man got out of the car, dragging a kid out behind him, and they went into the building across the street. I could hear the kid start to scream from inside Sean went to the door and it was locked and he told me to come get you."

"Which building," Tom Manfre asked her. "The one being renovated?"

"Yeah, yeah, that one," she said.

"Work there was shut down while they are waiting for permits," Foster said. Everyone had heard.

"I'm heading over there," I said. "Anyone wants in, let's go. Keep Tommy and Vivian toward the front. Manny!" I called to the bartender. "Call Captain Blake at the precinct and tell him what's going on."

"Done!" he called out. We left, and as we got to the entrance I separated the group and grabbed Dwayne.

"Group two, stay here so we don't overwhelm something that might not be a big thing. Dwayne, when we get in, if it's something that shouldn't be, come back and signal group two so they come."

I was in the lead, with Clarence, Carl, and Dwayne behind me. Tommy, JT, and Viv were behind them so we had someone that knows the law close to the front. Foster and some of the other guys were behind Vivian.

"Keep your eyes on that door," I said to the second group. Joe was at the front. "You see Dwayne wave, haul ass." Sophia had moved up to stand beside me. I was proud in the middle of what was happening. She was coming with me—well, she wanted to.

I whispered into her ear. "I know you want in, but you have to stay. If it is something bad I won't be concentrating on me or the situation, I'll be worried about you. I might get hurt or do something wrong. I promise when it's clear, you'll be there. It may be nothing."

"It's not, baby," she said, tears in her eyes. "I don't know how I know, but it's bad. I'll wait. I love you."

"I love you," I said to her. Four seconds later we were across the street. Sean was there.

"Boss, I could hear the kid screaming," he said. "Door is locked."

"Wait," Dwayne said. He ran to the lot which was only fifty feet away, popping his trunk with the remote. He came back with a big crowbar and he pried the massive door open far faster than I thought possible. We went in, two at a time. It was dark but not pitch. I tripped because I moved before my eyes adjusted. There were a couple of hanging lights that provided sparse illumination. There were stairs to the right and they lead to the second floor. Clarence was next to me. There was a hallway and double doors that weren't locked. We went through. We are all quiet and we all heard the scream. It was a kid. And it was bad. We couldn't wait for the cops. There were doors on each side of the hallway and another set of double doors at the end. Light and some indiscernible sounds came from behind the doors. We moved down, Viv and Tommy trying the doors as we passed. Most locked. Two were open, but nothing there but old desks. Terry and Clint took up the rear. That put me at ease. There was no time to go through the building properly, but we had all made that decision when we heard the first scream.

The double doors at the end were locked. Everyone waited. I tried them and Wayne moved forward with the crowbar. He leaned in and whispered to me, "I can't get it open without making noise and it will take me a bit. Anyone on the other side of the door will probably hear."

I debated looking for another way in and we heard the child scream again. Clarence looked at me and I nodded and said, "Fuck it." The group parted and he took a few steps back and hit the double doors at a run. All six feet eleven and four hundred plus pounds of him. The doors were not only not a match, they would have run if they could. They broke and flew apart and came off the hinges all at the same time. His momentum carried him past and he stopped himself from falling and we were in.

And it was hell.

4

THERE WAS an altar in the middle of the room and a small child no more than nine tied to it, surrounded by black candles. A boy. He was naked and crying and struggling to get free. A freak in a robe stood above him with a knife. There was blood on the knife and he was carving a symbol into the little boy's chest. There was about a dozen other people, of varying size, wearing robes. In the back, about forty feet behind the altar, were video cameras, a bed, a sex swing, and some couches. Behind that next to the wall were large cages, maybe dog kennels. There were a little boy and a little girl in one of them, holding each other. The little girl was crying, and the little boy was trying to comfort her. In the middle of all this horror I froze and then saw only what was on the wall. There was a satanic symbol. Red circles with a pentagram in the middle, and a goat with long horns superimposed on the pentagram. There were two upside down crosses on either side and something written in Latin underneath. FILII EIUS. I knew what it meant. It meant "His Children." The spell broke and I saw far off to the right was a refreshment table with all kinds of food and racks and hooks with clothing and equipment and things I couldn't make out. Refreshments. Good Housekeeping for Satanists.

We faced the monsters in robes. About two seconds had passed. Everyone was so surprised no one moved yet. For a second I could swear I saw my father standing over me in the cage he kept me in, my brother standing next to him, holding his hand. The freak that had been cutting the little boy, called out "Kill Them All!"

I don't know what you could call the sound that came out of me. Carl had said it felt like it shook the building. I flew at the altar and launched myself over it, at the freak in the hood with the knife. He got the knife in me a little ways as we crashed to the floor and the entire place erupted into pandemonium. There were gun shots and screams, loud crashes and the sound of me punching the robed figure as hard as I could. I lost count of the blows, and at one point he screamed out "Father!" He stopped fighting a few seconds and was barely conscious when I dragged him to his feet. His hood had fallen back and revealed his face. A large, average looking man with a brown beard. I drove my right thumb into his eye, and he screamed in agony. I grabbed his throat with one hand and whatever used to be his manhood below his waist with the other and I crushed both. He had to weigh what I did but the adrenaline-fueled rage in me didn't care. I was holding him up now. Sean had gotten the kid off the altar. I lifted the freak into the air and threw him into the altar with as much force as I could, and it shattered. I had no idea what I was doing. His body slumped to the floor as his head hit the stone floor and made a wet sound. Pieces of the altar lay around him.

The acrid, burnt coffee smell of gunpowder was in the room. Two of the freaks had guns. Vivian, Tommy, JT, and Foster had shot them. I had forgotten that Foster's gun permit had recently come through. One of the freaks with the guns had pointed it at Vivian or Foster and he screamed "Father!" Foster shot him several times. Vivian had been aiming at the other one. Carl, Dwayne, and Clarence went through the group like they were a shredder and the freaks were paper. My heart raced and blood pounded in my ears. One of the freaks tried to get past us and I tackled him, then picked him up off the floor and spun him around. I don't know how many times I hit him but he was out. It was like I had faded out and somehow we ended up across the room against the wall. He was falling forward and he was limp as I drove an uppercut at him that if it connected it would have killed him. Dwayne fell on me from behind and probably stopped me from catching a manslaughter charge. Despite his enormous strength I shoved Dwayne off me and grabbed the freak who had slumped to the floor and began choking him again. Carl got there and he grabbed one of my arms and Dwayne the other and they slowly pried me lose from the freak. They tried to pull me away and I almost broke free. They grabbed me more securely and Clarence appeared. He put his hands on my shoulders and looked down at me.

"Ham," he said softly.

Terry and Clint had caught the three that had cut and run at the door. One of the freaks running had a knife. It moved in a downward arc at Terry and then

Terry was moving so fast it was a blur. His knife moved in and out up and down like a sewing machine. Clint struck another. Hard. He might not be getting up again. The third freak dropped to the floor and covered up. I had paused as they held me and watched and turned back to the freak who had slumped now against the wall. As I struggled to get at him, Dwayne spoke to me.

"Boss," he said gently. "He's out cold."

I looked at him. I realized I was fighting my own people and I stopped. Carl and Dwayne held on, to make sure. I took a deep breath.

"They're all down for the count boss," Clarence said. "The ones with the guns won't be getting up any time soon, if ever. Cops are arriving outside. Ambulances, too."

I stared at him, not fully comprehending what had happened.

"I'm okay. See if the others need help. I'm sorry."

"For what, Boss?" Dwayne said and moved off. Carl looked at me.

"You okay?"

I shook my head. "Pal, please go get Sophia and the others." I just sat on the floor. Carl sat next to me and Dwayne ran back the way we had come. That part of the plan had gone to shit, once we heard the kid scream. Dwayne waded into the fray. In just a few seconds the rest of the crew came in and Sophia ran to me. I tried to get up. I realized I had blood all over the front of my shirt. Dwayne got back and unbuttoned my shirt and looked at the wound. It wasn't deep and probably not serious, but it had bled a lot. He saw towels in the corner of the room he went to get them. Sophia got to the double doors and ran to me. She cried out when she saw the blood. I told her I was okay.

As Sophia looked at me and we heard a metallic sound. Clarence had gone over to the kennel which had a lock on it and tore the door off so the little boy and girl could get out. They just moved to the back of the cage.

"Angel," I said to her. "Please help them. I'll be alright."

She did as I asked her to. Dwayne got back and his massive hands tore the towel into strips, and although the wound had pretty much stopped bleeding he put the strips against the wound. Clint and Terry had dragged two unconscious freaks back into the room. The first cops got there and Captain Blake was with them. I saw Sophia on her knees, talking to the boy and girl and they came out of the cage and held onto her. She was crying and holding them and saying it would be okay.

"I got to get up, Dwayne. Let me up."

He started to protest and I looked him in the eye and made him understand. "I have to."

He got me to my feet and I walked around looking. I looked at all the freaks. The ones that had been shot, two of them were dead. The third, the one who had been calling out "Father" died as I watched. Foster had shot him. As he was dying, he still called out, "Father." I stood at Foster's shoulder, who was watching him also. We watched as he exhaled for the last time, his eyes fixed on Foster. I knew Foster had been in the service and he had seen action. He seemed contemplative but not upset. The freak had been calling for the devil. Dwayne checked his pulse.

"He's gone," Dwayne said.

"Dwayne, the ones that Terry and Clint dealt with need to be looked at I can stay with that one," Foster said. Dwayne nodded and got up Foster knelt down by the one I had thrown into the altar.

"Terry can help," I added. "He has EMT training."

"He's in and out," Dwayne said in reference to the one I had taken out. "EMTs will get here soon," Dwayne said and he moved off to check the other ones.

Too bad he wasn't dead yet, but there's still time, I thought as I looked at him. He had been carving a symbol into that child's chest. Although I was not unhappy in the least some of them had expired, I also knew the more people the cops had to question the better it would be.

I started walking around and looking. I stared at the cages the kids had been kept in. I remembered the cage I lived in. Under the stairs in the house I had lived in with the monsters.

"Sweetheart, what are you looking for?"

I realized everyone had stopped, except some of the cops that were cuffing the freaks. They were all looking at me, concern on their faces. I looked at Sophia blankly.

"Honey, what are you looking for?" She was still crying.

"The monsters," I answered her. Her face froze and she stared at me. Everyone else was staring also. I took a deep breath and said to them all: "I will never as long as I live, call the two freaks that had me, mother and father. They are the monsters. I lived in a cage until I was rescued when I was eight. That," I said as I pointed to the satanic figure on the wall, "was on the wall in the building I grew up in."

She couldn't move because of the kids. "Come here, baby," she said to me. I stumbled her way. She held her arms out and I went into them. I felt the kids hold her tighter and the little girl held onto my leg. I knelt down and hugged her and when the two kids hugged me I hugged them back. I gently pulled away and looked at them.

"This lady, she's your friend. You are safe now. She will take care of you."

The little boy looked up at me. "Is that other boy okay?" he asked me.

I looked over in the corner. Sean was still with him and the paramedics were tending to him. He was awake and talking to Sean. I smiled.

"Yes. He is okay. He is safe now like you."

"They cut him."

"I know," I told the boy. "But we are going to fix them."

"Is my sister safe now?" he asked me.

"Yes."

"What if the bad people come back?"

"I won't let them," I said.

He looked at me, not quite sure.

"I promise," I told him.

He nodded. I smiled at them all, kissed Sophia, and got up and continued looking around. I looked at the broken altar first. My shoulders and my back hurt significantly. Just like in the movies. When I was on the weightlifting team, had I ever been able to put that much exertion in a lift I'd have scared the Romanians. I thought about the man I killed.

Two of them had been calling out "Father." I remembered hearing the freaks that had me referring to their master as Father. The Father. And the symbol. His Children. I'd never seen that anywhere else and I had made a study of the occult. How could it be here? It couldn't be a coincidence? The thing is, it's all bullshit. Satanism, for the most part, what you see in those old seventies movies, is bullshit.

"Dwayne!" Foster called out and I saw that the freak he knelt next to started convulsing. Dwayne got there in a few seconds but it didn't matter.

"He's gone," Dwayne said.

"Fuck him," I said. Foster came over and whispered to me that he was happy the guy was dead, too, but I should be careful. I nodded. He meant that I shouldn't cast doubt on the self-defense claim I'd make.

I walked over and looked at the one I'd killed. Dwayne and Foster stepped back a little. "You were calling for the Devil," I said to the body. "Well, you got him, freak." I spat on his body. "He was me. You got off easy," I said as I turned and walked over to the wall. The cops had come and started to move people around and tape off areas. I stared at the symbol. Foster came up.

"Ham."

I looked at him.

"What is it?" he asked.

"This symbol. I have seen it before."

"It looks common."

"No. The pentagram is. So is the superimposition of Baphomet on a pentagram. So are upside down crosses. But I've never seen all of that together. And the words. In Latin."

"What do they mean?"

"They mean "His Children," Satan's children. His servants, sacrifice, whatever. This exact symbol with this writing in Latin. The altar also. That exact altar and that exact symbol were in the basement of the home I grew up in. They were the monsters."

"Let's get you out of here."

I shook my head.

"Let's get you and those kids and *Sophia* out of here and tell the cops about what you know."

That got my attention. I asked him to get Sophia and the kids and I walked over to where Sean and the paramedics were, and the little boy. They had given him something to calm him down.

"This is my friend, Sam," Sean said to me. "And this is my friend, Ham," he said to the boy.

"Hi," he said. "Sam is Ham with an S. I like ham sandwiches." In the middle of hell, I burst out laughing. The little boy smiled at me. The two paramedics tended him. A male and a female. The male looked very young. I could see his eyes were red. The woman was busy.

"Well I do, too," I told Sam.

"They hurt me. They hurt my mom."

"I know, Sam, I'm sorry. They will never hurt you again."

"I know. Sean told me so. He saved me."

"Then you can be sure that's true."

"Yeah," he said.

5

It was all over the news the next day, and also on the internet, which in 2008 wasn't as big as it is now. The *New York Post* had a headline that read "HEROES" and had my picture and Foster's picture. Other headlines read: "Horror Show" and "Cult of Evil."

The byline in the post read: "Nightclub manager and head of security tangle with Devil Worshippers and Pedophiles. A confrontation that began when a nightclub crew broke in on a cult of freaks that were cutting up a small child ended up with a number of the freaks dead and others in custody.

It was Monday night, and despite the Gates of Hell opening only last Friday, we needed to get the meeting done. The club was closed and everyone was there. Under normal circumstances it would be weird for at least a few people to miss it but after what happened, everyone was there.

Everyone was on the main floor seated and I used the stage where the sound system was.

"Thank you all for coming. I first want to say to

everyone that was here Friday. During something that was a horrible as one could imagine, you all proved yourselves to be heroes. I am honored to work with you all and you are part of my family. I will never forget what you did and how great you were. My thanks and my love go to all of you. The key word there is family. I will always regard you as such. There's a saying, you can't be counted in unless you can be counted on. You all passed the only test required to be called family. You were all heroes."

Foster stood. I paused. He addressed the group, whom he sat among like he was a soldier and not the general he was. "You were the hero, Ham. It's a privilege for us to have you as a leader. While we were all trying to figure out what the hell was going on you launched yourself at the sadistic son of a bitch." He stood on his chair. "God Bless you, Ham." He started clapping and all the rest joined in. I felt a tear form in my eye and I quickly brushed it away. I'd had no idea they were going to do that. After a long while they stopped.

"Thank you. I wasn't alone, that's for sure." I cleared my throat. A reporter had contacted me and had told me he was doing an article about what happened and apparently he'd been tipped off by someone as to who I was and what had happened. I gave him a few quotes and didn't talk about my childhood.

"There will be another news article tomorrow. It's going to be about me. I tried to dissuade them but it's done. I wanted you all to know this from me, not the papers. First of all, I told them and insisted that they take a verbatim quote from me and use it and I'd answer some of their questions. I'm sure you can understand, it's not something I enjoy talking about."

I paused and looked over them. They all waited. Sophia was in the back and she had tears in her eyes. She had just come from visiting the children. The little boy that had been on the altar had been placed in protective custody. His mother had been involved with the freaks but when they wanted to use him in their ritual, she refused. They killed her in front of the boy. Some of the surviving members had said he was special to them and he might still be in danger. Captain Blake told me that he was spirited away. Bernie Keri had something to do with it, he'd told me on the QT, but no one could know about that. Bernie had come to the club on my second night there and we had gotten to be friends.

The leader of the group had not been present. Worse, no one knew who he was. Most of them called him Father. Now I wondered if the freak I'd killed had been calling him or Satan. Blake also said some of them referred to him as "The Vessel," and here was the freaky part. The man I killed was the second in charge or command I guess you'd call him and he knew him, but he was dead. They were looking into him, hoping to develop information. As far as the article, they were going to write it anyway. So, I insisted they put in I said we helped those children.

For the hundredth time, I wondered how the hell it was the same exact symbol the monsters had. I had made a study of the occult. The college I'd attended actually had courses in it and a degree. I'd never seen it. Never. Nowhere except where I lived with the monsters. It's a very complicated thing but Satan Worship is kind of like a Christian Construct.

"You're going to read about it anyway, so I want to

tell you first. When I was a child, the monsters, as I told some of you last night I won't ever call the freaks that had me mother and father, abused me. Sexually. They filmed me being raped and sold copies. And they sold drugs. They murdered my little sister. They let their friends do the honors. I was born, they said, to be a servant of the Devil. The monsters might have believed that but for the most part the ones that paid for time with me just liked hurting kids. I was kept in a cage until I was almost nine. Always hungry, often cold. I had a brother, but he was treated differently as he was first-born. He was being groomed to be a priest I guess you'd call it, like the monster people would call my father was. My brother was also abused but in different ways. He disappeared with someone who was the money behind it all."

I paused there. I heard how upset some of them were but like I told them, this would all be in the papers tomorrow and the old news articles of when I was found and rescued would likely be floating around again, too. Just what I wanted to see. I knew some freaks would read it and want copies of the videos. It couldn't be chance. With my history, a cult operating across the street from me? Long odds. But the symbol cinched it. The detectives in charge of the case had told me it was almost a certainty unless the symbol was found to be more common than I thought. It wouldn't be. There was a man, he funded the monster, he was the real leader. My brother had been with him.

Because it was no coincidence this happened across the street, I was terrified that the connection to me would hurt Sophia. I was already feeling like I should let her go. I already loved her and I didn't want her to be in danger because she was with me. My insides crawled a little when I thought about that. About losing her. I looked at her and as sad as she was she smiled at me. That smile alone almost made me forget everything. Almost.

I talked for a little while longer and told anyone that might need time off because of this they had it. With pay. I would cover that myself. One of the club staff came up and whispered to Foster. He nodded, smiled at me, and left. I told them again how much I appreciated them for what they did and I walked over to Sophia.

"That was beautiful," she told me.

"Well, thanks, babe. They deserved it and other stuff they had to hear from me. How are the kids?"

"Good, they're good. I wish I could take them. I spent the last day just crying thinking about them."

I thought about them and what they would be going through. The other little boy, too. I thought about my mother and father. I knew that if it wasn't for them, at the very least I'd be a drunk or addicted to something else. At the worst I might have been doing what those freaks across the street were doing. No. I wouldn't have gone that far. But this constant feeling I have that I don't deserve what I have, to be happy, all the doubts—they'd be ten times worse.

I looked at the tears running down my woman's face. I knew that the short time we spent in hell would have a lasting effect on her. And those poor kids. The way the foster system worked. I knew then.

"Can we go to my office a minute?" I asked her. "I need to talk to you."

When we were in there I sat in the client chair opposite hers and I held her hand. I asked her if she still wanted to be with me. She got mad. I explained. She got madder. "I'm with you, fuck them." I never heard her curse before. I smiled.

"Then I have some questions for you. And a few things to say."

She nodded.

"I love you. I love you very much. In such a short time I can't imagine not being with you."

She placed her hand on my cheek and leaned in and kissed me very softly. She still had tears running down her face but her expression was different.

"That's good because you're stuck with me."

"Forever?" I asked.

"Forever."

"Would you say we are going to go through with what we talked about? That we are going to get married?"

"Yes."

I dropped to my knee and withdrew the ring. "Then marry me and let's adopt those kids."

6

WHEN WE WENT DOWNSTAIRS we saw Captain Blake and
Bernie Kerik talking to Foster. We went over and joined
the conversation. After they got over the surprise they
shook my hand and all kissed Sophia. I told them what I
wanted to do. Kerik took us aside and left Captain Blake
and Foster to talk. He told us he should be able to help
cut through the red tape with a few calls. And just like
that it was all in motion.

In a matter of days, background checks were done.
We moved into Sophia's house and we had the kids. We
were their foster parents to start but immediately we
started the long process of adoption. I felt, believe it or
not guilty in some ways. There were so many people
trying to adopt kids. Very few of them had the police
commissioner show up at a crime scene where we
stopped the sacrifice of a child. Most people would go
into debt and not have a friend in a very high place. Our
process went smooth and still cost us about twenty-five
grand.

Kerik told me years later he knew, because he knew

what happened to me and the type of man I was, that I'd be good for those kids. "I affected things on a large scale he said. I've seen some awful things in my career, but that," he said, jerking his head in the direction of the building across the street. He didn't finish, he just shook his head. "If I can help those kids get with you," he said, "I did something good."

The dogs got close very fast. They were soon best of friends. I didn't have a lot of things I was I suppose a minimalist or I lived a Spartan lifestyle at least when it came to possessions. We'd be getting the kids in two days.

We were downstairs in her living room watching TV after we'd been intimate upstairs. In conversation I used that word, intimate, she giggled and turned around and looked at me.

"I'm curious can I ask you something?"

"Sure."

"You are a very sexual person. You spend a long time making sure I feel good and you know things and do things that are really sensual and erotic, but when you talk about it, you get red in the face and you look down. You're doing it now!" she said, laughing. "You do things to me that bring me to the point of fainting but then when we talk about it your face gets flushed."

"It's a complicated answer," I said. "I was aware of sex when I was young because of..."

"Okay," she said to put me at ease when I had trouble talking about it.

"So the normal curiosity a kid has was heightened with me. And a few other things happened, like when I was doing chin ups one day when I was eleven I had a —" I couldn't finish.

She laughed. "Oh my God your face is red again. You had an orgasm?"

"Yeah," I said sheepishly. "But you have to remember I was very, very shy. I also felt, I guess, dirty, because of what had happened when I was a kid. I had huge anger issues and because I'm introverted I kept a lot inside. That's why I was so involved in sports and martial arts, stuff like that, helped me burn off a lot of energy. But I was still curious and early on I had feelings, desires I guess. I never really spoke to any of the therapists about that. One of them asked and kept asking and I felt warning bells go off with the way he talked about it. I had just told Mom I didn't like him and she took me somewhere else."

I took a sip of water. "My friend and I would go to Waldenbooks and read in the self-help section all about sex. What to do how to do it, how to," I stopped and my face got really red.

"It's okay," she said and laughed a little. It didn't matter that she did. I knew she wasn't laughing at me.

"It even told you how to practice," I said as my voice dropped lower. "Because I was so shy, I wasn't with...I mean, I didn't go all the way with a woman until I was almost twenty-one. But, she never knew I was a virgin."

"Wow," she said.

"And because I feel so strongly about you these intense desires and wants, I guess, are even stronger. Most kids that are abused are sexualized. I knew this in my teens so I decided to make it into something good."

"How many women have you been with?"

I laughed. "I don't keep count, but I did become very active. Run security at a club and you get a lot of offers. The thing was, anyone I developed feelings for, and by that I men strong feelings—I can't be with someone if there isn't at least affection," I said. "But I'd keep everything inside and I couldn't talk. I'm surprised, sweetheart, I was able to talk with you. I guess I felt so strong about you I had to."

She turned again and looked at me. "I am so happy you did."

I kissed her and that kind of started things up again and we ended up on the couch and the floor and resting again, watching TV. She was tracing her finger on my shoulders and traps and looked at me.

"You're really strong," she said.

"A lot of people are strong."

"No, that's not what I mean. I was taking with Carl, he said you cleaned and raised?" She looked at me questioningly.

"Pressed," I told her.

"Over 400 pounds, almost twice your weight. And you snatched almost that much. He said very few people in the world could do that much."

"He exaggerates a little."

"A couple of the guys said you threw that man, that night, like he was a rag doll," she said quietly.

"I keep strong and I also do strongman exercises to keep it interesting as well as the weightlifting, or Olympic lifting as some refer to it. I also had rage infused with a massive amount of adrenaline."

"Carl said you could close a number three gripper, that you were really strong, and he is huge and powerful."

I smiled. "He is. And he is being a little kind. I can close the three with my right hand but not all the way with my left yet. He can almost close the 3.5 with both hands. That's well beyond me. Anyone can do what I've done, with hard work and dedication. I don't work out for how I look. I train to be strong. For work."

"Have you fought a lot?"

"You mean for real?"

"Yeah."

Yeah," I said. "And I boxed and wrestled and now do martial arts, it goes with the territory."

We were quiet a bit.

"Sophia, what happened to me, I live with it every day. I think about it less as time goes on but I do think about it. It affects me in a hundred different ways. What I've tried to do is turn that to an advantage. Make something good out of it, but if you watch you'll see over time, what I mean."

"Can you tell me a little? Or does it bother you."

"No," I said. "It doesn't bother me." I thought a bit and took a breath.

"They would tell me I was stupid. Retarded was the word they used often. I'm glad that word is out of style, it should be. They'd call me slow. I heard those words, years after. I sometimes think that of all the things they did to me the emotional abuse was the worst. Knowing they didn't love me. So to prove them wrong I studied very hard, I started reading and I read everything I could get my hands on. I'd talk with my dad about the stuff I read." I smiled.

"I read *The Great Dialogues of Plato* in the fifth grade. I still have the book. I wanted to use it for a book report. The teacher told me it was too advanced and I explained it to him in class. He mocked me a little and I got a detention because I told him just because he couldn't understand it, it didn't mean I couldn't. My father had some talk with him and the principal. He apologized. So did I because my Dad made me understand I had insulted him in front of his class but he also knew I didn't start it."

I saw I wasn't boring her so I talked a little more. "I wanted to know I would never be helpless again. I worked out, I took boxing and martial arts lessons, wrestled. My dad taught me to shoot. I'm sure you noticed I shower a lot and I don't have much in the way of body hair. One day when the freaks came over to rape me, because my—" I caught myself. "The monster hadn't bathed me for over a week and the woman kept repeating that I smelled bad." I laughed bitterly.

"I offended the olfactory sense of the grown woman who was going to rape me, while it was filmed. When I was reading an article in a magazine about ancient Egyptians, I read that they shaved their hair, body and head, because it was more sanitary. I started doing that. All of these things affect me to this day and I decided when I was a teenager that if they were going to affect me, I wanted to make something good out of it. Because most of the time I was starving, my first year with my parents I gained a lot of weight. One of the kids at school called me fat. I talked with my dad about it. He told me about eating properly, and how it could help make me strong. I threw myself into that. Food became fuel, although I learned to eat what I liked also. I—"

She interrupted me. Sophia had come over to me and hugged me. I felt her sobbing as she did and I felt bad. I held her tightly. I didn't want this. I wanted her to know why I had a few screw loose but I didn't want her to feel bad. I told her that and she told me to hush.

"If you want to tell me I want to know," she said. "I just feel so awful this happened to you."

"It's okay, its better now. It will always affect me a little. We are all the sum of our experiences and what we do with that. It's up to us what we do with what happened." I smiled. "And now you are helping to make it better.

"The one thing that bothers me most," I said. "No one knows anything about what happened to my brother. He used to sneak me food sometimes and once he gave me a blanket when it was cold. The monster called him "The First" as in first born. There was a man who was friends with them. The people that had me. My brother often went with him. Looking back with adult eyes they treated that man the way a catholic family might treat a priest. They treated him with respect, not fear exactly."

"The cops had to look for him?" she asked.

"They did. Hard. But remember this was a long time ago. No cell phone or internet connections for leads and this man was extremely cautious. The woman monster, she didn't even know his real name.

"They learned very little about that man, or my brother. Walter Hertman was the cop that rescued me. He led the investigation, but there were FBI and state cops involved also. They sold child pornography to people all over. It made headlines, and when they found us, they had been getting ready to do some filming and there were other people there. They only knew the mystery man through the Monsters."

She nodded. She looked so sad. But she wanted to know.

"What happened to your mother, I'm sorry, the female monster?"

"Died in prison. Lung cancer," I said. "I was told she had found Jesus. She had sent a letter to Mr. Vachss, when I was over eighteen. He contacted me. He told me that she wanted to see me. I asked him if I had to. I still remember him telling me, "hell no," in that voice of his. I asked him if I had to forgive her. He told me no. It was a pernicious lie that in order to get better or to move on I had to forgive people that raped and abused me. If I wanted to, fine, if I didn't, fine. I asked him if I should and he told me that was something I needed to decide. I told him I couldn't and we talked about it for an hour.

"He did this great interview on Oprah Winfrey and he addressed that lie. You forgive mistakes, something people do when they slip up. That the people who tried to force you to do that, force you to forgive with the threat of your salvation at stake, they were just imitating the abusers, forcing us to do something we didn't want to. I did wonder if I she might not have been a victim also. I mentioned that to him. He was careful to let me make the decision. I asked him if I could send her a letter through him. He said sure. I thought about, talked to my parents about it. Well I told them, anyway. They asked what I wanted to do. I told them they were my parents. The only mother and father I had ever had. I told them I decided not to talk to her. She died a short time later."

"Did you ever regret it?" she asked me.

"She used to help make the videos and on one occasion at least, that I can recall, she was my co-star. I have no regrets."

"Oh my God," she said. "I'm so sorry."

"It's okay, it was a long time ago. It's not hard for me to talk to you about it, it's just that, I never seem to tell you all of it and then something like this comes up and I tell you, and you feel bad. I don't want to keep hurting you."

"Oh, honey, I love you. I want to share it with you, to listen if you want to tell me about it. Don't feel bad, please don't."

"It always feels like," I started. My eyes teared up.

"Like what sweetheart?" she asked me.

"I feel like I don't deserve this. That I don't deserve you. Like something will happen. I feel like I don't deserve this life."

"Did you talk about this with the therapist you told me about?"

"Yeah, and she said it's common for people who have gone through what I have to feel that way. I still see her once in a while."

"Well listen, you don't have to tell me anything but if you do, I want to know. I want to share this with you. I mean, does it help? When we talk about it?"

"Yeah, it does. Then I feel guilty because it hurts you and I—"

"Stop. I want to know. Okay?" she asked. "Ham, if I needed or wanted to talk to you about something that hurt me wouldn't you want to listen?"

"Of course!" I said.

"Well then why can't I be there for you? Please let me be there for you. You do deserve to be happy and I feel so lucky that I make you happy."

I sighed and swept her into my arms and held her as tightly as I could without hurting her. She fit just right.

She held on to me, too, and we just stayed like that a long while.

"Do you know why my mother named me Hamilton, I mean besides I sometimes think to get me into a couple of fights?" I whispered into her ear.

She laughed. "No, why?"

"She is religious. She wanted to give me a powerful name because in her heart she thinks it will help protect me. She knew it would be "Ham" for short. She named me after Noah's son. My father didn't want me to have his name because he had a lot of trouble when he was a kid. He said anything but Noah. Soooooooooooo she named me Hamilton."

"She meant well," Sophia said as she giggled a little.

"Yeah. She did. I still had at least nine fights because people called me Ham and Cheese."

Everything fell into place with my family and work. The kids were great. They adjusted so well. Sophia often gave me credit because I knew what they had gone through. But it was her. Her love for them. Her love for me. Our personal relationship grew stronger and more intense. We had missed the toddler years, changing diapers etcetera. No missed sleep. We talked about having more children and we agreed that if it happened it happened and we'd be happy either way.

I'd made a full gym in the basement with a safety rack and an Olympic Platform. It saved me time. A heavy bag, a treadmill. I got her and the kids to use them. One thing about our home was besides the dogs, I had weapons in every room. Often it looked like the Katana I had on display, which you could do surgery with. Mag-lights, knives, and a few guns. I made them unreachable for the kids when they were young, and I showed them how to access them and use them when they got older. I spent time with Sophia at the range. When the kids were older I taught them about the firearms and I made them understand how pulling a trigger was one of the most serious things anyone could ever do. I took them to the range also and spent a lot of time explaining that they were to keep the family safe and they should never talk to their friends about them or anyone else. I made the forbidden fruit not forbidden, and removed the curiosity about it. My daughter could outshoot most men at fourteen.

Our lives were great. I loved my family. We had been together ten years and I still craved Sophia's body all day long. It didn't take me long to miss her when she was gone. I worried that sometimes I might love her too much and I was around her too much. I asked her about that once and she smiled and told me she hated it when I was gone. I Lived to see my kids come home and I felt good beyond words to do for them what my parents did for me. Both my parents and Sophia's and her brothers and sisters were in our lives. The kids loved them all. They took me in their hearts. My parents and hers actually went on vacation together. They hit it off. I couldn't be happier.

The problem of me not deserving it though, that still stayed with me. And the fear that I didn't deserve it and that it would all be taken from me intensified rather than abated. And memories. Sometimes they would just intrude and I couldn't force them out. I still had nightmares sometimes. I've woken a number of times maybe once or twice a week and Sophia would be there, her face sad, her hand on my chest or blotting my forehead as when this happened I'd often break out into a sweat.

I would never miss working out, or the range, or whatever martial art I was working. I had the best possible security system and cameras. I had the house swept 4 or five times a year. Still, despite all these measures I worried about the safety of my family. Both my therapist and Sophia thought it would be a good idea for me to write what happened. I took their advice and wrote, which you know, if you're reading this.

One day a couple of years back I had to go upstate to look at a club. Business was great it grew steadily. I had the luxury of being choosey about the work. I wouldn't turn it down but I had to have the freedom to run it the way I saw fit. Anyone could go to any of the places we had and see how good we were. I built the reputation on the work of my people, and I took good care of them, and I was able to do such a good job because of them. It is that simple. When I went upstate, I had ten locations and two estates in the Hamptons. I now had partners and associates. I'd always listen to them and factor their experience into my decisions.

After the trip of several hours, I ended up not taking that job. I'd need more time than they gave me to properly find the ops and man the place and they objected to my drug policy, which was if I caught you and it was weed, you put it out. If it was the hard stuff you were gone. If you were selling you were gone. Don't get me wrong. Trust me on this, if you had no drugs it's unlikely you'd have a nightclub, but you had to make an effort to control it. We now had a PI license as well as a security license but didn't do much of that work. State regs, in order, I imagined, to increase revenue, had changed. I had someone that was qualified to give the required classes which were near useless. And anyone working for me spent a lot more time than that training and learning, and there was always a trial period.

————

WHEN I WAS UPSTATE, outside of Washingtonville, I was eight minutes away from the Dungeon. What I call the "home" I "grew up" in. I had told myself there was no need for me to go there. Yet I ended up there.

It was falling apart. It had never been sold. It was almost a certainty that it was referred to as a haunted house. And it was. I was just intending to pass by, but I found myself in the front yard. The front door was open about six inches. The interior was dark, and when I pushed the door open the grey light of an overcast, fall day reluctantly shone in. It made the room brighter, but it was almost like the light didn't want to be there, or felt it didn't belong in that place. It was fall after the foliage had dropped and winter was reminding you it was not far away. It was cold, bitterly so. I wouldn't go in the building. I wouldn't call it a house or a home. I told myself I wouldn't go in, but, of course, I found myself inside anyway. There were signs of use. Kids from the area probably went there and hung out. There were couches that looked like they had been thrown away and dragged in. It even looked like the fireplace had been used recently.

The iron bars of my makeshift prison were still there. Efficiency was one of the monster's traits. Economizing the available space, the monster made my cell under the stairs by removing the cosmetic paneling and putting up iron bars. I lived in that cell for the first eight years of my life, under those stairs. The filthy mattress

—if you want to call it that—I used to sleep on was still there. A bowl also, I'd been given water in. I felt hot and began to sweat. I was afraid but also angry. Very angry.

There was a huge hole in the middle of the ceiling, and it lined up with another hole that, had there been illumination, you could have seen through into the second floor and its ceiling. I wasn't curious even though I had never seen the second floor. When they used to film the freaks raping me, if one of them complained that I smelled bad, they bathed me in a dog tub in the basement. The water was always ice cold. Although once, it was hot enough to scald me, punishment for failing to move quickly enough. I stared at the center of the living room where the monster had died. An inch of dead leaves lay on the floor, scattered beer bottles and cans. There was one torn up converse sneaker. I knew it wasn't mine; they had never given me shoes or sneakers, and it had to have been left there after the investigation had been completed. There were holes in the walls, and I could hear now and again the sounds of small animals scurrying around behind them. Surprisingly, most of the windows were intact, and it would be fairly warm if the door was closed. There was that smell of rot, and I could see water stains on the sheetrock. All the paint was gone.

As I stared at the middle of the living room floor, I remembered the cop picking me up and taking me out. Walter Hertman was his name. We still stayed in touch to this day, probably the only two people left who exchanged actual letters through the mail. I stared at the spot on the floor where the monster's body had lain after Walt had shot it. As I stared and remembered, the thing that called itself my father began to materialize, there on the floor. On the front of its shirt, a dark red circle began to expand where Walt had put three rounds from his .357 only inches apart, center mass. The huge knife the monster had raised above his head was now on the floor next to him. His eyes glassed were over.

I remember staring even as Walt covered my eyes and hugged me. I told him "My dog," and I reached for Rex. He was a puppy the monster had killed the night before. It strangled my pet while I watched. As I stood there, a tear rolled down my face on the left side. The monster had left Rex's body for me to play with, laughing about it with his friends. He told me if I was good, if I behaved myself when they made the video, and if I did as I was told, he'd bring Rex back. You see, I had not come to him right away when one of his freak friends showed up with his freak wife, the night before. He had gotten the video equipment out and was setting it up joking and laughing with the two freaks that had shown up. Others had arrived earlier in the day. I knew what they were going to do to me. I knew how much it hurt, and I hid under the blankets holding Rex. Pretending not to hear them and making believe I was sleeping. That's why the monster killed my dog.

As I turned to leave, the monster stood there, before me, smiling. I knew I'd see it when I turned. I was not afraid. I wasn't surprised. Somehow I just knew. He was smaller than me now, and I weighed fifty or sixty pounds of solid muscle more than him. I didn't shrink, I didn't cower. It was the opposite. I felt the muscles in my chest and shoulders ripple and bunch up. I clenched my fists. I flexed and loosened the muscles in my body and felt the strength and power that I had built up for years.

Every time I picked up weights, punched a bag, ran up hill, sparred, and all the times I fought in the bars I worked, I built my suit of armor—armor between him and me. Each workout made it thicker. Every time I went onto the mat, into a ring, fought in alley, I made my armor stronger. I would never be hurt by the monsters again. I was no child now.

"Happy to see Daddy?" I heard the monster ask. Its lips didn't move. I heard it in my head. But that was its voice, just as I remembered and still heard in my nightmares.

I spat in his direction. When I spoke to it, I pronounced each word and took my time so the meaning would be understood. "You were many things, none of them good. But you were never my father. I am the Adam of your labours, but I am not what you wanted me to be. Fuck. You." I said this as I walked through it and toward the door.

"You are mine. You are his. You are his servant."

I stopped, but I didn't turn around. "I am happy you're dead. Although sometimes I almost wish you were alive, so I could kill you myself. It's a shame you didn't suffer more."

I kept walking, and I didn't turn to look. I didn't know if I'd see him in the doorway watching me. I didn't care. It didn't matter. It couldn't hurt me anymore. As I walked to my car I did not know if it had been there or if it was just my imagination. It didn't matter. I got in the car, backed out and left. The monster was dead, and my life—my wife and children—were waiting for me.

I GOT HOME LATE that afternoon. I kissed Sophia and held onto her very tightly. She knew something was wrong. I told her it was nothing. I went into the basement and spent half an hour punching the heavy bag until my arms were rubber and I was spent. I sat with a towel around my neck and my head bowed. My wife came down. I could see she was worried, and I hate that I made her worried, that I made her feel like that. She knelt on the floor next to me and looked at me. She was sad. I said no when she asked if she could do anything or if I needed something. Her eyes searched mine. I took a deep breath and told her what had happened. She put her head in my lap and I stroked her hair.

"I'm so glad that you didn't take that job, so near to that place."

I actually hadn't thought of that. I'd still have taken the job and I wondered what impact that might have one me. The kids wouldn't be home that night. It was Friday, and they were sleeping over her parents' house. Next week, they'd see my parents. We got up and went to take a long hot shower. I'd washed everything but my back, and as I reached for the long-handled brush, Sophia opened the door and stepped in with me. My wife is a living and breathing work of art. I gazed at her and she smiled and blushed a little, as she always did.

"Let me, baby. Let me take care of you." She washed my back and pretty much everything else. She dried me off and then herself and led me to our bedroom. We lay on the bed and as I kissed her mouth and then her neck and worked my way downwards she gently stopped me.

"Let me take care of you," she whispered. "You always take care of me, let me make you feel good."

And she did. We exhausted ourselves and lay there

after. Her head was on my chest and I'd faded in and out of sleep for a bit and then eventually I slept. I had one of the dreams again. I woke with a start and she asked if I was okay. I told her I was. Her hand caressed my face.

"Still thinking about it?"

"Being in the Dungeon?"

"Yeah."

"Yeah."

"Can I ask you something?"

"Sure," I said.

"Do you think he was really there?"

"I don't know," I said truthfully.

"Were you afraid?"

"No," I said thoughtfully. "I know that sounds weird. Did I see a ghost? Was it in my imagination? Was the catalyst of me being back in that place enough to make me hallucinate? I honestly don't know. I remembered that day, the day Walt found me. I felt rage, anger. He killed my dog. I know that he hates the fact I am not what he tried to make me. And it just kept running through my mind I was not a little boy any more. He can't hurt me anymore."

She held me. Her body shook a little and I realized she was crying. I gently raised her chin and brushed the ears from her eyes.

"I'm sorry, Sophia. I shouldn't have said so much."

"Oh, Ham," she said, crying a little harder. "You have so much pain inside you. Of course you should tell me."

My eyes teared up. "No, it just makes you feel bad. Both of us shouldn't..." I trailed off.

"I'm your wife. I want to know. I just wish," she said

and looked away for a second, "I just wish I could help you."

"Sophia, you do help. You make it better. I need to stop talking about it so much. I need to move on from this. It's always something else, my sister, my dog, my brother. I wish—" I sighed. "I wish I could move on or get some kind of closure. When I passed a gas station I thought about getting a few gallons and going back and burning it to the ground. It's like there's never closure. Even the kids seem to be handling what happened to them better than I handle what happened to me. I have to find a way to stop it from, no to stop myself from thinking about it. But I can't. Most of all, if I knew where my brother was, if he was alive or dead," I trailed off and shook my head.

"You tried to find him, you hired people, even the FBI looked for him when they got involved and they couldn't find him. I wish you could find peace."

"I'm at peace when I'm with you," I told her.

She kissed me again and my hand found her breast and I held it gently. She pressed into me harder and I then I was inside her again. She looked into my eyes until it became too much for her and she cried out and closed her eyes, trembling and whispering things that only she understood. She was medicine for me and I overdosed. As my soul bled she became part of me and closed the wounds.

Things were tenser for me than usual for a few weeks after that, but everything eventually got back to normal. Well our normal. For the most part I was grateful for the life that I had. A few bad dreams here and there, the occasional feeling of dread was as usual, the worst of it. My first eight years had been horrible but honestly, if I knew that I had to do that to have the life I have now, I would have. I sought solace in her as I had come to do. That just meant I'd spend even more time with her. That we would be intimate more and it would be very intense.

Well there is one more thing that came out of it. Sophia's house, now our home, was beautiful. It had plenty of room. She insisted on putting me on the deed. A week after visiting my old prison, I was looking at the stairs in our house. We had a front porch that had originally an outside porch. Then they had closed it off and made it a front room you got into from the living room. I was quiet one day and looking back and forth at the porch and the stairs. I don't know why I had never noticed it before, but the stairs were open underneath. She knew I didn't like closed spaces much. Some years ago, at a friend's, my son had ventured under the back steps into a small basement, like an old root cellar. I went in to get him and I looked pale when I got out. I had asked her once if we should think about opening the front porch and just making the living much bigger. She thought it might be a good idea but we really didn't talk much about it.

A few days later, Ted Lanzi, a guy that was a partner in one of the clubs I ran security at, had bought a place in Atlanta and asked me if I could go with him for a few days and take care of the security. I knew some people down there and told him no problem. I was there for four days. When I got back, the house had been transformed. The porch was gone, the wall shored up. It made the living room much bigger and wood paneling that matched the beautiful hardwood floors covered where the space under the stairs were. There was an inset door so we could actually use it for storage or even make a safe room out of it.

I can't describe how touched I was she would do that for me. Even the usual feelings that I didn't deserve this failed to diminish what she did for me.

I haven't written here for a while. Although Sophia has told me she thinks this would be a great book, I only really write here when there is stress. It seems to help. I see a woman I know for therapy about once a month, although in truth I hadn't seen her for almost three months. Things were going well. Work, the kids, my Sophia. Everything went well for a long while after. It was all good, until yesterday.

7

STEPHANIE WAS at her friend Joanne's house. They were working on some kind of school project with two other girls. Although she had passed the test for her driver's license and it appeared I would have to use our entire retirement savings to pay for the increase in our insurance with both kids driving, she wasn't comfortable driving at night yet.

I was happy she was possessed of enough common sense at her age to be honest about that and I was always happy to pick her up, if she needed it. Elias, her brother, wouldn't have done that. I had a rule from when they first started to get more freedom. No matter what they were doing, whether I would approve or not, they could always call me for a ride. If they were out with friends and they felt something wasn't right, the deal was they call and I get them, no judging, no punishment and they promised they'd call me.

I was a father first and a friend second and that was not always easy. Like any parent, the idea of my kids being hurt or in pain was difficult. But part of life was pain. Elias wanted to go into the Golden Gloves last year. I had taught him how to box, among other things and had brought him to a boxing gym a friend of mine owns. And I told him, he had to know what it was like not just to hit, hitting is great everyone is ready for that, but he had to know what it was like to get hit and if he was ready to keep going after that, he could do it.

One of the pros did us a favor and moved around the ring with him. Just before the end of the round he gave Elias a decent shot. It knocked the kid back a step and then he went right back at the guy. When we got home I told him if he woke up tomorrow and he still wanted it he could do the gloves and we'd start getting ready for it. My wife got up at three to find me sitting on the bed and crying. Partly because I had engineered it so that my son got tagged with a good shot and partly because of my pride in him, the way he went right back at the guy. When he woke up he found me and told me he still wanted it and he placed fourth in the super middle weight division. He hadn't decided if he was going to compete again next time. But my pride in him, and how he dedicated himself was enormous.

I was taking my time Steph had texted me she needed to be picked up about ten. I had left at nine-fifteen and it was only a twenty-minute drive. I took Manor Road and was reflecting on the stories people used to tell each other about serial killers and devil worshippers in the woods near here. Although Andre Rand had eventually been convicted of killing a child and he may have been the inspiration for some of the stories there evidence about a black mass had never really been found.

I had a CD in and listened to the Luciano

Pavarotti, whom I had met once in the city. Fortunately, I was driving slowly, a bit under the speed limit, so I didn't hit the girl who ran in front of my car. She was young. She was naked at least from the waist up as I could see her breasts. Her eyes were wide and wild there was blood coming from her nose. I think she screamed, but I wasn't sure. I had to cut my wheel and jam on the brakes to avoid hitting her. She tripped and went down hard, the front of my car ended up off the road but the ground there was flat. I was out of the car as soon as the parking gear had been engaged.

She was on the road trying to crawl away, crying. She had panties on. I yelled what any idiot would have yelled.

"Hey! Are you alright?!" She kept crawling in the same direction of the road, trying to get away. "Stop! Hey, stop!"

I got to her and she cowered and put her arms up in front of her. I opened my palms and said as soothingly as I could I wouldn't hurt her. She looked at me and struggled to understand. She must have realized I wasn't trying to hurt her and she wailed.

"Please, please help me, they're going to kill me. They hurt me. Please help me."

"No one is going to hurt you, I promise." I cursed myself for not carrying my firearm. I rarely carried it. I could have had it but I didn't. I bit my lip as I scanned the area. I saw headlights in the distance coming this way from the opposite direction I had come.

"They'll kill me, please, please," she trailed off, weeping.

"Sweetheart, it's okay. Give me your hand." I

reached down to her. She took my hand and as I helped her up she cried out as she put weight on her right foot.

"Can you walk?"

I saw both of her feet and legs had a lot of cuts and scratches. She bled from a lot of places and her arms and upper body also had cuts. Her right foot was ballooned up to twice the size it should have been. Maybe she twisted her ankle, could be a break.

"Branches," I said to myself, looking at all the cuts. I scanned the area again nothing. The car was closer. "Can you walk?" I asked her again. I could sense movement in the woods. At least one person was moving in our direction. There was a street lamp that illuminated the roadway. Much further in the distance I heard someone shout.

"Oh, it hurts, it really hurts."

"I'm going to carry you to my car okay?"

"Yes, okay, please don't let them get me."

"I won't. I'm going to get you out of here, sweetheart, no one is going to hurt you," I told her. "I promise."

She heard my voice then and knew I meant it. I scooped her up and carried her to my car. I got the passenger door open and put her in, and closed it. The car as it passed me was close enough for me to see the two guys in the front. I waved both arms and began yelling to them, they ignored me and kept driving, I cursed under my breath. I popped the trunk and grabbed a blanket I kept there and gave it to the kid. I knew for her sake I had to get her out of there, I'd give anything to put hands on the people that did this, though.

Yeah, so when they overwhelm you they get the kid

back, the voice in my head said. Get her out of here, dope!

I scanned the area again. Nothing. The sound of movement had stopped. And then I knew someone was watching me. I was illuminated by the street light. They would be able to see me, but I couldn't see them. I saw another set of headlights, way off in the distance. They were moving slowly, the curves in the road were significant. I got to the car still scanning the area as I did, I reached down and locked the doors before I got in. I had one foot in the car and I stared in the direction where the sound of movement had come from.

"Please, please let's go," the girl whispered urgently.

I was about to get in and a figure stepped out of the woods on the edge of my eyesight. Tall, wearing an ornate robe. The hood hung over the face but it sat wrong. It sat in a way that indicated his head was deformed. I couldn't have seen the face from this distance, what I guessed was about a hundred feet away from me. But even from here I could see the robe. And I knew that I had seen those robes when I was a child. And again, ten years ago. The girl saw the figure and screamed. She began to cry and shake and she started saying, "They're here!" over and over.

My heart raced, and thoughts boomed through my brain. How?" This can't be. This girl was terrified. I began to burn with rage. This was no coincidence. I had to get the girl out of here. Yet the rage burned hotter. Control it, don't let it control you. You'll find him/them again. I told myself. Get the girl out of here. If I could get my hands around that bastard's throat, I'd know everything I needed to.

"Can you drive?" I asked her. The figure started

striding forward, but he stopped about sixty feet away. He was tall, broad shouldered. Not likely a woman so it became a he in my mind. Fairly big. Head cocked forward so now that I couldn't see a face, even though I was close enough because the hood hung over it.

"Can you drive?" I asked her again forcefully.

She never answered. She just kept begging me to take her out of here. I had to get her out of here, I knew, I had stayed too long already. But I wanted to put my hands on the visage before me, he that wore robes like the monster that imprisoned me had worn. Like the freaks wore that night in the city, when they started carving the pentagram into that baby's chest.

"Here!" A voice bellowed, as the figure turned around and called out into the woods to let the other pursuers know where he was. "She's here!"

It turned back toward me and took the hood down. Whoever it was wore a mask. An expensive black leather mask and I saw immediately why the hood sat so oddly on his head. It was the horns. The mask was the face of a goat. Baphomet.

"Come to us, Ham," said its voice.

It wasn't a shout. It was just loud enough for me to hear. My jaw dropped. He called me by name. Was this all done for my benefit? Had this been planned? Was the girl in on it? No, she was terrified and I was hurting her and risking her life. We needed to go. But how? How could they time it so the girl ran in front of my car at that precise time? I looked at the weeping girl. I heard a voice cry out from the woods, "Where are you?" Not close but not far, either.

The freak in the mask spread his arms wide towards me. "Come home, the father calls you back."

I could no longer feel the fear I should have. I had to go or the rage would take me. The girl had to come first.

Before I got in the car, I stared at it maybe another two seconds. My heart was pounding. I thought it would beat right through my chest and it seemed to drown out the cries of the girl.

"You will see me soon enough, and when you do," I called to him, my voice raised just loud enough for him to hear me. "You will wish you hadn't. I will tear your fucking heart out and show it to you. After I tear off your fucking Halloween costume."

He laughed and bellowed behind him again. "Here! She's here!"

I got in the car, started it, and shot down the road. We passed the car I'd seen in the distance. I should have gotten her the hell out of there faster, I knew. I also knew this was not a chance meeting. It could not be a coincidence.

We barreled down the road. Whoever it was that might have been chasing her, I didn't figure going up against them and risking them getting past me to her again would be a good idea.

"Who was trying to hurt you, sweetheart?" I asked her. "Who was that man?"

"Please, we have to go. There were a lot of them and they had knives, please."

I nodded, watching the rearview mirror and the woods on both sides. As I drove I called 911. When the operator came on I told her what happened. I also told her the girl said there were about a dozen of them and it wasn't safe for us to stay. There were stores less than a mile away I told her where they were and that I'd meet the cops there. I told her too it looked like they tried to murder this girl and we needed the cops there now. I saw headlights behind me and coming from the other direction.

"Sweetheart what's your name?"

"Anitra."

"How old are you?"

"I'm going to be eighteen."

"I have a daughter about your age. I promise you I'll make sure you are okay. The cops will be there." I scrutinized the headlights behind us in the rearview mirror. They moved steady and slow, not trying to catch us. I got to the light, which was red for us. I saw no cars coming from either direction, blew it, and turned left.

"Anitra, do you live on the island?"

"Yeah, with my mom and sisters."

"Can you tell me what happened?"

"I went to a store. I parked in the lot. I, I, I shopped and I went back to the car and that's all I remember. I think someone hit me, the back of my head hurts and I threw up before."

She cried softly as she talked. I could feel the rage building in me. If only there had been another car that stopped, I could have...that would be a smart idea alone and unarmed.

"Okay. Can you tell me who tried to hurt you?"

"Uh uh," she said. "I woke up and I was on this table. They took my clothes off and there was candles and people in robes, like chanting. There was big picture, on the wall, like painted on the wall it had spotlights on it, of a goat or a man that looked like a goat inside of like a star. Like the thing that chased me."

"It was a man honey. A man in a mask. A monster, yes but a human monster."

"They all had masks on. And robes. They hurt me. When I woke up it felt like they had been doing things to me." She started crying.

"That happened to me when I was a kid," I told her. "It's not your fault. And I promise you, it hurts now but it will get better and if you ever need me for something you'll have my number."

She leaned over with the blanket on and pressed her head against my shoulder. I kept my right hand on the wheel and gently rested my left hand on her head. "It's okay, child," I told her.

8

THE COPS WERE ALREADY THERE, a lot of them. I was shaking, and the sergeant I was talking to seemed to think it was because I had found the girl. I told him I could take them back to where I found her and that I could be of help. She described it as something ritual in nature and I was familiar with things like that. One of the degrees I had obtained was in Occult studies.

"What do you mean, Mr. Grant, like they are devil worshippers, like that?" he asked.

I nodded. "She mentioned a symbol, like a painting or picture on a wall. It's got to be in the old farm colony. I remember exactly where I found her and it has been years since I was there. It's all that made sense. It was the only structures in those woods."

He made notes as I talked to him. I took a deep breath. "Detective, I'm sorry, I'm a little off. What did you say your name was?"

"Sebastian, Bill Sebastian. I'm a second grade NYPD Detective."

"Yes. Detective Sebastian, you need to know a little more." I told him about the man in the mask. About the city over ten years ago now. He was thoughtful. I held back on telling him he knew my name.

"The actual number of Satanic or Satanic related crimes is small. I find it hard to believe this could be chance or a coincidence."

"Exactly," I confirmed. "But of those most are rumor or just freaks that like to hurt children using it as a front for what they are doing or a justification. And this garbage, it's a contrivance, a construct. I have a feeling though, these people believe."

"What do you mean, a construct?"

"It's," I paused. How did I explain this? "You know those movies that were big in the seventies, devil worshippers, cults, etcetera?"

"Yes," Sebastian said.

"That's Hollywood taking a Christian construct. The Church was competing with Paganism. They accused people of devil worship and things like that. There is no evidence people ever worshipped the Devil, the Fallen Angel, Lucifer. It may be some did but that was what was used as a weapon. The Church wanted Christmas to be the holiday that replaced Pagan holidays. There were entities, evil spirits if you will, that some people worshipped. Some were benign. The Church didn't want competition. When we broke in on those freaks hurting that child in the city, the altar, the color of the candles, it was all wrong. Even on those rare occasions where it is real, in the sense that they hurt or kill some- one, it's like a kid, listening to heavy metal, on acid made up what they are doing. These people that partake in devil worship are—" I searched for a way to explain it better. "You know how you guys look at wannabe cops?"

Sebastian nodded.

"Like that. A fringe movement. I'm not saying you didn't have people believe that stuff but it's a fringe."

He nodded. "But still, they could be dangerous."

"Absolutely."

"Yet here you are and," he said.

"In the middle of it. Before you say it, Manhattan couldn't have been a coincidence, either. No one could find the connection," I said.

A reporter who introduced himself to me as Frank Donnelly asked me a few questions and asked if he could contact me in the future. I told him he was welcome to but please understand this had been some-what disturbing. I asked him if he was going to put the girl's name in print, and he told me not if she was a minor and if she wasn't it was up to her. He agreed to wait until a future point for us to talk. He turned to walk away and stopped. He turned back and looked at me.

"Sir, your name is Hamilton Grant?"

"Yes."

"The same from that incident upstate and the inci-dent in Manhattan from about ten years ago?"

"Yes. I'd prefer we not talk about that. I will tell you whatever else that I can."

He stared at me for a bit and nodded and walked away.

Detective Sebastian came to me and said they were ready to go back about a dozen or so officers in different cars went back. I sat in the front of the detective's car so

I could better see and in a short while we had parked as much on the side of the road as we could, where the girl had run out in front of my car.

I had called home and Sophia had made arrangements for our daughter to get home. My heart was racing. I knew what we were going to find and I started wondering how. Then I caught myself. No. Go on facts. Wait. We found a path not far from where the girl had run onto the road. We walked along the path. The full Moon helped. I was actually thankful for it, not only did it help with the light, I may have hit the girl without it. About twenty minutes later after a slow pace we found the buildings. It didn't take long. The candles on the altar were still lit.

The buildings were a maze. I had been there once before. There were dozens of paths and ways in and out of there. You could go from building to building. The room we were in was big. It had been cleared of the century's worth of junk accumulated. It was clean. There was a generator. I saw the video cameras. I took a dep breath and inhaled. I went inside myself, and, brought myself to the level I needed to be.

"Detective, may I use your flashlight please?" I asked him.

He handed it to me. I ran the light over the cameras and equipment. The large dog kennels that were empty. Was that good or bad? Did they have kids here and they had a chance to escape with them? I ran the light over the walls. First one, then a second, and on the third I found what I knew would be there. The Symbol. The pentagram with Baphomet inset, the two upside down crosses on either side, and the Latin writing underneath. Someone started taking pictures. They stopped when I walked in front of them, as if I was in a trance. How? How could this be? An impossible coincidence when we found the kids. And now? Again? No it was like I thought even before the figure stepped out. It was no coincidence. It was not chance.

"Mr. Grant? Sir?"

"I'm sorry, Detective Sebastian. What was your question?"

"Are you okay, sir?"

I shook my head. I opened my mouth to explain but couldn't. I kept staring. One of the other cops had come over and stood by me.

"Do you know what the Latin inscription is, Mr. Grant?" she asked me. "Have you seen this before?"

Rowley was her name. "I've seen it before. Twice. Once in my childhood and once about ten years ago."

"Is it common?"

"The symbols are but not the way they are incorporated. Nor the writing. And again," I said. "This is make it up as you go along stuff."

"Do you know what the words mean?"

"Yeah." I nodded. I shook my head and took a deep breath. "It means, His Children."

"Whose children, Ham?" another cop, who had come up, asked me. His name was Orlando. I recognized him. Steve Orlando. He used to work for me before he became PD. I put my hand on his shoulder and he squeezed it.

"Satan's."

By the time I had gotten home, the sky was getting light. I sat in my home office/den. Sophia had come in. The kids were in bed. She was wearing the robe I had gotten her last Christmas. I sat in the recliner and she slid into my lap. She kissed me and nestled in and lay her head on my shoulder. We were quiet a long while.

"What are we going to do?" she asked after a long while.

"I don't know."

"I'm afraid."

"Don't be. I promise it will be okay nothing will happen to you or our children."

"What about you?"

"I'll be okay."

"How can this be a coincidence?"

"It can't be," I told her. "Whatever the reason is, it's by design."

"I don't understand." She was crying softly.

I stroked her hair and told her it would be okay. I would find out, I'd find out and this would stop. Whatever I had to do, I would do. I would protect my wife and kids. I'd not hesitate to do anything that needed to be done. I needed answers. I needed to keep my family safe. I thought about the girl that had run in front of my car and of the kennels. I needed to make sure no more children were hurt.

I held her for a long while. She fell asleep soon and she slept soundly in my arms. I held her as long as she slept and let my arms go numb. This was going to stop. I would not allow this to be in my life anymore. At some point Sophia must have woken up and somehow she extracted herself and covered me with a blanket. When I woke and slowly got out of the chair she was in the room in no time as I was stretching a little. She had hot coffee which smelled like heaven. It was early still. I thanked her, took my phone, and found Commissioner

Kerik's number. When he answered, after exchanging pleasantries I told him everything. He told me the Police Chief in charge of the Island was a good man. I told him I had no doubt if he said so but I wanted someone looking out specifically for my family and to help me find out what was going on. He told me he would call the man he had in mind and mention I was a personal friend.

"He can make it rain," Kerik told me. "He is a good man, and he will give you his all."

He gave me the number and told me he would text me the info as well. I asked him the man's name again.

"Jimmy Creed," he said. "Give me a few hours to see him. I'll actually be passing through Staten Island shortly, and I have time. I'll call or text you when you should call him."

"Very good. Thanks, Bernie."

"If you need anything, for Sophia or the kids, call. I mean it."

"I will."

"Take care, Ham."

Upon calling Jonathan Creed (Jimmy? I wondered), I got his secretary first. Apparently Bernie had spoken to him. He was on shortly and asked when I'd like to come in and meet. I told him it was urgent and I'd see him as soon as he could see me.

"I am in the middle of a few things, work kind of exploded today. You can come now but I may need to stop and deal with a few things while you're here, or you can come this evening."

"I understand, Mr. Creed. I can be there in about an hour."

He said that was good and hung up. I got on the

computer and did some research. I saw some of the things he had been involved in and what a few people online said about him. I liked what I saw. I went to my documents and began writing and bringing everything up to date.

PART II

CREED

PART II

CREED

9

AL MCLAUGHLIN CALLED ME. He was a client and an old friend. His brogue sometimes manifested itself when he spoke. His parents had come over from Ireland not long after he was born. He was also the best civil defense lawyer I had ever worked with. He lived to be on trial and could be irascible between them. If he was calling on a Sunday night, it would be work related and his wife would be pissed at him.

"Hey," I said into the speaker. "Let me guess, you're calling me from church?"

"I wouldn't know where it was," he said.

"What's the good word?"

"I got a hot one in from Lyon Property and Casualty," he said. "They called me a few minutes ago they are delivering the case files to my office in the morning. Trial is two weeks out. I already got the gist but you tell me what's going on after you read the files. I got authorization for you and I can do what I want. Its red flagged for fraud and they want to go to verdict."

"Wow, that is uncommon these days. And who the hell is calling you on a Sunday?"

"Wait until you hear the details because this one is a doozy. I'll be in at ten. Can you meet me?"

His firm took up four offices upstairs and two secretarial spaces. "I'll be there at nine sending the troops out."

"Great."

"Tell Donna and the girls I said hi."

"You got it," he said.

We hung up. Doozy would be an understatement.

He called me back in five minutes.

"Hey, I left the files for the case in the conference room. The plaintiff's name is Sorenson. If you get the time feel free to get a jump on it."

"Done."

10

I WAS UP EARLY MONDAY, cardio, stretching, breakfast, shower, and dressed and in the car by seven-thirty. It had taken a long time to come back from being shot and that was delayed when it was almost completed and I threw hands with Todd. There was still and probably would always be the occasional twinge. I could probably be expecting arthritis in my later years and I damned sure knew when it was going to rain. But today, I felt good. I dressed in good jeans, a black dress shirt, and a light brown suede sports jacket with black loafers. Mariano had been after me to change what I carried. When I got in I removed the Kimber .45 and put it on the shelf I had made under my desk. I got a legal pad and turned the Keurig on. It had been a gift from Cory. I was certain having that machine in the office would end up with me getting caffeine poisoning.

I liked trial prep. It was almost never life or death. Insurance companies paid much less than other clients. I got ninety an hour plus expenses on these cases. I would always do the prep myself, which consisted of reading the files, the medicals, the background of the plaintiffs, information on witnesses and the accident that caused the suit to be initiated. The summons and complaint, something called a bill of particulars, depositions that had been taken, any investigation that had been done. Most importantly, the insurance company information, case or file number, and claims rep for billing and reports.

I had brought trial prep into the new century, before the new century. As far as I know a number of things I did as standard procedure were firsts. I did a background check on the plaintiff, the witnesses, and the treating physicians as well as our physicians. I often found little gems that way. I once gave an attorney information that got the suit dismissed because the plaintiff declared bankruptcy and did not list the lawsuit as a potential asset. New York State law in that instance would dismiss the suit. I found doctors that had convictions for perjury, lawsuits against them for malpractice. I frequently found all kinds of information people never thought to look for. Al had, with some help from me on occasion, gotten over a dozen defense verdicts, meaning nothing for the plaintiff but bills from their doctors for testifying. We had also often brought the monetary awards down much lower than the case was worth.

I would make a list of all the medical, employment, and other records that had to be subpoenaed, some of which we already had, so that they could be offered into evidence. The key there was knowing the ones you wanted and knowing the ones you didn't. Copies had to be furnished to opposing counsel, some subpoenas for city and state agencies would need to be so ordered, meaning the judges' signature on it or so requested, if they were federal agencies.

I would also line up our client (the insured defendant) to have them in court, our doctors (their doctors would say the plaintiff was a cripple while ours would say he or she was fine) and any witnesses that supported the defense.

Right off the bat I'd have four hours just for reading the file, an hour for preparing the subpoenas, an hour for background research. I read the file from seventhirty until nine when I met the investigators I had working that week in my office. I had two criminal cases going. Sly Turner who retired from the NYPD as a detective was working them for me. He had done buy and busts for thirty years for both PD and on numerous occasions the feds.

Investigators and ops handling various things for me stopped by and reported, picked up checks and got directions. Mark DeFazio and Judy Sandomierski two very old friends, although only Mark and I aged, stopped by. Mark gave me a box of Line of Duty Cigars, a new brand. They set up a business along the lines of Black Rifle Coffee and the company made generous contributions to very worthwhile charities. One of them was Tunnels To Towers, a charity set up by the Siller family in memory of Stephen Siller. When the human refuse attacked the twin towers, Stephen, a firefighter ran through the Brooklyn Battery Tunnel to get there with all his equipment. He died there like so many we still mourn. I'd have bought those cigars if they tasted like tires, but they were damned good.

After he retired from PD, Mark became a sales rep for Line of Duty despite my best efforts to recruit him. My office door sealed so I locked it, and we violated New York state law and smoked a cigar each and sipped some port for a while. Damned good cigars. I got up as they went to leave, and Judy turned and caught me watching her walk out.

"After all these years, you still check me out Creed?" she asked in mock despair.

"Hell yes," I said. "Lady cops always have their own handcuffs, and the view sure as hell ain't changed."

She laughed and came back, leaned over the desk and kissed me lightly.

WE HAD a quick cup of coffee, and I mentioned some things that were happening next week I'd like them on if they were available.

I got back to the conference room at nine-thirty. Dolores and Norina were hard at working doing billing, second and third requests for payment, and transcribing reports from our investigators, changing the language and putting it on our stationary. When they were done with that work they would go through case files and update them. See what had and had not been done, etc.

Al texted me that he was running late he'd be there about eleven thirty. I had the file done by then and asked Dolores to stop what she was doing, I gave here legal documents with captions and my notes so she could do the subpoenas and the letters to our insured and our doctors.

I actually had time to start running the database research on the plaintiff, Richard Sorenson. I used four different databanks all of who drew on credit headers for their primary source but they differed in sources for their secondary and tertiary sources and sometimes they came back with different info. I ran motor vehicle record searches, checked for prior law suits.

I checked for malpractice suits and disciplinary actions for their doctors and ours. The only witness in this case was Sorenson's mother. And she was our insured as well. He was suing mommy.

I reread the file folder that had the fraud investigation.

Al walked in with a coffee for me as well as himself from the coffee shop down the street. He dropped his briefcase on the table and sat and looked at me.

"Doozy was not an understatement," I said.

He smiled. "Run it for me."

"Once upon a time, Dickie Sorenson's father actually made a table saw. Let us pause here and say that is something that neither of us could do if our lives depended on it," I said.

"Fuckin A!" Al said.

"Young Dick, then after getting out of the Army, gets into the New York City Sanitation Department. Dick every so often uses his father's tools and work bench etcetera for "projects." I made a note to find out more about the projects.

"Papa Sorenson," I continued. "Getting up there in years, puts young Dick in charge of his decent sized estate and it appears young Dick contributed to it and bought some properties. One fine day, he was working on a "project" and was using the aforementioned table saw. Which incidentally did not have an on and off switch and was operated by turning the wall light switch on and off. He apparently got something jammed in it and turned it off, without unplugging the saw. Momma Sorenson or Poppa Sorenson, depending on when the story is told and by who, walks in and asks him if he wants a sandwich and sadly in doing so, flips the light switch on."

We both shook our heads and chuckled a bit. I know that sounds cruel but you can't get through this stuff without finding humor.

"And?" he asked me.

"Fingers everywhere," and we burst out laughing.

"And why, Sherlock, is it that Lyons isn't just throwing money at this case to make it go away?"

"Oh, I saw the initial offer was 500K. As they re-attached the fingers and he was eventually able to go back to work. However, sadly, it was red-flagged for fraud after they gave at least four?" I asked him.

"Let's just say multiple," he said.

I nodded and continued. "Multiple versions of events. One cannot help but think the later versions are designed to put all the liability on one or both of the parents. This makes the insurance company think there is considerable chicanery afoot and they decide to take it to trial whereas before, knowing insurance companies, they would have gone from five hundred to at least seven hundred and fifty K, considering the severity of the injuries, and settled and have been happy to do so."

"Well done," Al said.

"Only in Staten Island," I said.

"And what are the problems we have?"

"You're hired by the insurance company to represent Momma and Poppa and you must do so to the best of your ability, they are clearly going to try to hurt you and I would say cooperation on their part will be somewhat lacking. The case is worth some coin. The injury is bad. If he couldn't return to work, I venture they would have settled no matter what flags because he'd lose 30 years of wages from a city job with great benefits and guaranteed raises etcetera."

"Good."

"And what may I ask will your position be?"

"Not a damned clue yet."

"Nice," I said, nodding my head.

"But you're right, it's a shit show. They are going to fight me all the way on this."

"How good is the plaintiff's lawyer?" I asked.

"Good."

"I already have the employment subpoenas being done, select medical records subpoenas and letters going out, and Dolores is calling the parents. The trial date is marked final for 2 weeks from now," I said.

"Is it?"

"Yeah," my friend replied. "And judges work forty hours a week."

"Considering it is NYC agencies we need some records from, I'll get a judge's signature today and get the subpoenas served tomorrow. I'll start following up on them next week and I'll send copies to their legal department saying the trial date is firm and we want the records properly certified and in court. I'll also ask the judge to sign off on us copying the records once they are in, so you have a copy ASAP. I notice Lyons never got them from the authorization, which they sent in twice?"

"Three times. And follow up letters," Al replied.

"No real surprise there," I said. "City agency."

"Nope."

"You want to grab lunch?"

"You buyin'?" he asked.

"Hell yes."

The girls had the subpoenas done when I got back from lunch, and feeling restless, I took them and headed to St. George. I went to Supreme Court and the TAP part was closed. That is the Trial Assignment Part. Judge Minardo was in charge of it. He was put in charge of the court because it was a mess. It wasn't after he was in there for a while. I knew him and I liked him. Judge Gigante and Judge Kuffner were in and any judge could so order the subpoenas for me. I always put Honorable Justice Presiding in lieu of a name in case we needed it done and it was an emergency and the judge on the subpoena was not in. Once signed the subpoena formally became a court order.

Judge Kuffner was speaking with several attorneys in chambers, but Bob Gigante was free. Bob was everything a judge should be. He was kind and strong, he had intelligence, common sense, and compassion all in proper amounts. We kissed each other on the cheek, which I told him the first time he did that, I thought it might have been the kiss of death thing. He never came to the company Christmas Party at Luger, or allowed the courtesy of anyone buying him lunch. He knew about the appearances of impropriety.

We sat and Mrs. Lanzi one of his assistants brought us both coffee. I had grown up with her sons, Mike and

Ted. She was still attractive and kind didn't do her justice. Their dad, was one of those hard working old school Italians. He was still strong enough to lift the back of a small car. As I sipped my coffee I thought about Mr. and Mrs. Lanzi and the two good men they raised. I was fortunate in my life, in the people I knew. I rarely saw them these days, Ted worked for a company that owned night clubs and Mike was in advertising. Ted had tried to get me on board supplying security but everybody loved the guy whose company was handling it now.

The Judge did me a favor and called Judge Minardo and asked if it was okay to sign them in his stead. Minardo made some good natured crack about that damned Jimmy Creed flexing his muscles and calling in favors but he allowed it. He knew how the city agencies were. He also in addition to being a friend, had known my uncle who had christened me with "Jimmy."

The subpoenas now bearing a Justice's signature (we called them Judge, but in this state the technical title of a Supreme Court Judge was Justice) were considered to be a court order. I took them back to the office and had copies made. The girls called a couple of the people we had working per diem for us and they picked up the subpoenas and the fifteen dollar checks that were made out to the agencies or people that accompanied the subpoenas. The idea of the fee was to cover transport or postage if it was for records. If I had reason to believe a person we were serving might not have a checking account, we used cash or I made the check for twenty to cover check cashing. In theory. It also served as proof of service.

The next day all the subpoenas were served, and

copies sent to the plaintiff's attorney as was required
and the court as a courtesy. I told Dolores to speak with
Mrs. Sorensen every other day till the trial started and
to document it. The affidavits were done and ready to be
signed and notarized. The research was on going. I had
found a few interesting things like business names at
Sorenson's addresses; that deserved further inquiry.
And the following day, at nine thirty we got word the
case was postponed. I looked at my calendar book. We
only had a couple of active cases. It was Wednesday and
although I preferred being busy we could probably use
the time to go through and update old cases, and maybe
have a few easy days.

Whenever you see the PI on TV, or in the movies or
read about him, he has one big case he's working on. It
wasn't like that, at least for me. Although in fairness
most of those people were solo guys and I ran a small
agency. The reality was if you were only handling one
case at a time odds are you were hurting for money. But
we had been damn busy. We were more than bucks up,
if nothing came in for months we would have no problems financially.

It was often a feast or famine business. So you took
the work when it came and if you were jammed you
found a way. I often thought about doing more security
work, which had a lot of logistic difficulties, to bring in
more cash flow. Process serving, which was something I
only offered as a service to investigative clients, was a
nightmare. Most politicians, in both parties, sucked.
There are more refined and classy words but that is
what expresses it best. The average New York City voter
was becoming more of a disappointment to me. This
city even at the best of times was hard on the small busi-

ness people. The new regulations regarding process service, entirely useless, recommended to the New York City Council by an activist law group, (and if you walked into a gathering of either aforementioned entity, they could never be confused for a MENSA meeting,) made it almost impossible to do the work and charge reasonable fees.

The activists had lamented that there was too much sewer service, after some nutcase had been caught generating affidavits for over 300 serves in a day. If the Starship Enterprise was beaming you from place to place you couldn't do 300 in one day. But he had been caught, the serves voided, and he was tried, found guilty, and imprisoned. So actually the system did what it was supposed to. An educated idiot lamented in testimony that "Real New Yorkers" would want their day in court. And wouldn't duck service. Yeah. People with debt collectors hounding them, drowning in debt are eager to get served. What that idiot and the law group did, along with every barely functioning moron in the Council that voted for the changes, was screw their own constituents.

What they would finally do was show up in court, say the serve was bad, the debtor would have a lawyer there and rather than hash that out with a traverse hearing about the service, offer them a big discount, they'd pay a fraction of what they owed, and the debt which had likely been bought made someone some money. Now with the GPS logs that option would fade. And they also screwed another group. Usually a single mom with a deadbeat dad barely making it would show up. I'd take the serve, sometimes do it myself and not charge them, or send one of my guys and charge them cost. That was dead now. Although I still did that sometimes and Jeff pretended he didn't know.

Well with all that being said, I looked forward to a few light days. I hadn't been to St. Peter's to see Mandy recently. Maybe I'd take Friday off and catch up on some reading, or call Rhea.

"Anything else, Jonathan?" Dolores asked me as she sat there and scribbled. I had found her through a friend. She was retired in her late sixties. She took shorthand, and that was just as cool as it sounded. She called me by my given name and although she worked for me, frequently it felt like it was the other way around.

"No, but let's keep an eye on this one, just a feeling. I'm hoping it's not a crazy week," I said. "We only have two days left."

"Well, you can always hope," she said amused.

Of course that all went down the tubes. Fifteen minutes later Jeff came in to my office because we had a rush criminal case for a young attorney, who had just left the D.A.'s office. I'd had lunch with her a few weeks ago and I was impressed with her. She was bright and knew things usually people with a lot more experience knew. And she was grounded in reality. She called and we put her on speaker. She asked if, even though this was her first case, we could take a little less on the retainer. It was some poor schlep. She'd only done a phone consult but he was a referral from a good source. He was driving a friend's car and got caught with some heavy weight in the trunk of the car. She believed him when she said it sounded like he didn't really know. Her client would see us ASAP, and she'd pay the retainer. I put her on hold and called Sly Francis. He dropped what he was doing and came right to the office.

He sat in the client chair forty-five minutes later and I gave him all the info. We called the client and Sly told him he was on the way. He stood, his broad six foot three frame towering over me. He had this almost perpetual smile on his face. His dark skin broke to reveal gleaming white teeth when that broad smile took his face. Which it did often.

"I'll go easy with you on it Jimmy," he said.

"No need," Jeff said. "She'll be a good client so charge normal."

I agreed. "Well hell, you don't have to tell me twice," he said as he left.

We then got two more trial preps, an appointment Jeff would take for another crim case in the morning and an order of protection that had to be served on a person who tended to be violent.

I went to work on the preps, Jeff vanished, and it became another busy day. Sly called a few hours later.

"Boss, who said this guy was a citizen?"

"Attorney. But she hadn't met him yet. She was trusting the person that referred him."

Sly had a rich deep laugh that made you smile. He had a great sense of humour and his intelligence was impressive. He had survived doing high end UC work, buy and busts for NYPD and the Feds, for years. I'd seen him shoot one and he wasn't just impressive, he was scary good.

"Well, uh, I got a few things to tell you."

"Pray tell," I said.

"First off, he is a trafficker. No one knows him, it must be that somebody ratted on him and they found five keys of meth at an apartment he kept, not in his car. We are talking major mover of product here. He goes down half the city is in withdrawal. He is also likely to state there are huge errors in the police reports insofar as date, time and place of arrest."

After he gave me the lowdown I asked him for the guy's number. He said the guy was waiting for my call and he was standing outside the guy's residence, which was not his residence. I spoke with him, told him to give Sly a check for 10 grand and keep himself available. He didn't hesitate in the least. I then called the attorney and asked if she had gotten the retainer. She said no, hadn't even discussed it. I told her she needed to get 25k out of him and explained.

"You are fucking kidding me!" she had exclaimed. "I was misinformed. I'll give you your normal retainer."

"Not necessary. We got it from him. The standing legal retainer we have with you allows that but we still work for you."

She was eternally grateful and we likely now had a lifelong client. I always looked out for the attorneys. At least the ones that looked out for us.

Then we got a surveillance in for New Jersey, and that took an hour to put in place with one of my ops that had a Jersey License.

Jeff came into my office and while I had been on the phone Pat Brackley had called to let us know he'd have a crim case that night. He, Joe Mure and his father Al were doing. Jeff said he was leaving and stopping off to meet someone that had made an inquiry about security services. For the most part we farmed that out, but if we were involved we made sure to know what the job was and keep tabs on it.

"I need to get going, son," he said to me. "Susan is busy burning a roast and I want to get home while it could still remotely be considered meat."

"That's mean!" Norina called out.

"But sadly true," Jeff said.

He was gone about five minutes when the priority line lit up. We had started it a few months ago when we were handing something high profile and needed a direct line to the office for a client to call. We decided to use it for special situations. The thing was, there were no special situations at the moment. Dolores answered. I could tell by her voice and what she said she was a little puzzled.

"Very good, sir, please hold I will get Mr. Creed."

"Jonathan, there is a man on the phone. His voice is familiar but I can't place it. He says he knows you and would prefer not to say his name on a phone line."

Not exactly a first but still unusual. I smiled at her and told her I'd take it. Who doesn't like a mystery? I reached for the phone and my right shoulder twinged. When that happened I had a thousand different thoughts and memories in a second. I moved them aside until after the call. I'd never not spend a little time thinking of her when memory pushed in. It was the least she deserved.

"Creed," I said as I picked up the phone. I resisted saying, "Creed, Jonathan Creed." But, I did consider it.

"Hi, Jimmy. I hope you recognize my voice, I need to see you about something ASAP and I don't want anyone to know I'm back in New York. But it's important."

"I remember the voice, sir," I said. "When and where, I'm free now."

"That park, off victory Boulevard, on Royal Oak. I'm there."

"Same spot?"

"Yeah."

"There in five."

I assured Delores I would be okay because her radar was up. I left quickly out the back after grabbing my sports coat and drove to the park.

11

I GOT to the spot where I had met him a few years ago. It had been a while since we spoke. I remember at the wake, there was a beautiful arrangement sent by him and his wife. He had been overseas at the time. He was talking to a couple of women who had young children in strollers that recognized him. I smiled. So much for low profile. I knew him well enough that he'd not ignore anyone coming up to him.

He saw me and waved me over and apologized to the women and walked toward me. We shook hands and then he hugged me. He apologized for having missed the wake.

"It's good to see you, Commissioner," I said to Bernie Kerik, and I meant it.

I had met him after his release as I knew his attorney and handled a few things for him. I will never forget reading his trial transcripts and to this day there are few things that I've read that made me physically feel ill. That was one. He had made a few mistakes if you even want to call them that. Had he not been close to someone running for president it never would have mattered. There was clear impropriety in his trial transcripts from the judge and the prosecutors. I was home, and I saw the second plane hit the tower on television. I knew five guys that died that day, all good men. I remember feeling crushed and broken after. You used to see the towers at Victory Boulevard just after Forest Avenue. Those cowards, those miserable cretins took down my towers. I remembered them well, standing proud in the distance when the ships sailed into the harbor for the bicentennial.

I had heard Bernie talk once about 9-11. After we met, I had dinner with him to brief him on something I did for his attorney, Tim Parlatore. He invited me to go with him after, to an event he was asked to speak at. I saw the pain in his face. I saw his eyes tear up as he recounted what happened to friends of his. I remember feeling better when he was on television. And I despised a system that would sacrifice a man like that, for politics. All the fools screaming for reform in a system where they had no clue where it needed it. People who had never met a criminal or been in court. Many of those people had no problem with selective political prosecution.

He had just gotten out and was rebuilding his life and I know it was hard on him. He still insisted on paying me. The next day I tore that checkup and mailed it back to him.

"How are things?" I asked him.

"Can't complain," he said. "Busy, a lot of work coming in."

"It should be that way, Commissioner, I'm glad

things worked out. I was happy when you were pardoned. Long overdue."

"Thank you, Jimmy. A friend of mine had just told me about that case you were involved in and that world title bout of yours."

I rolled my eyes and exhaled. "That was not something I'll forget anytime soon."

"How'd it end up?" he asked.

"Plea deals. How they usually end. The muscle turned on the baby rapers and the woke princess, he spent a few weeks in the hospital, and got probation after. Him ratting them out was the nail in the coffin."

"Damn," he said. "Not bad, kid, two members of congress and their backer. Damn."

That brought a smile. "I never thought of it that way. I did do the public a service," I said. "You know how it is with child protection, Commissioner, both parties claim to love kids, neither does anything to help, and here we had the truth. The rising star on the left watched a child repeatedly raped by her boyfriend and backer, and because the overall good she would do makes sacrificing the kid okay. And the conservative pillar of morality, backed by the same handler regularly rapes children with his buddy."

"Damn straight." He looked at the sky for a bit. "Jimmy, I'd like to refer you a client."

"I'm honored Commissioner." I said. "Be happy to send you something back on it, or if it's a friend discount them."

"He is a personal friend. A good man. He is well off and wants to pay any courtesy you could grant him would be appreciated but you don't need to work for free Jimmy. He doesn't mind paying, it's more important he gets help. Its..." He trailed off. "Well, I'll let you draw your own conclusions."

"Tell you what, Bern," I said. "I'd give you at least a 25 percent commission of the net. Let me take that off for him, tell him you didn't want it, and I'll discount it to him. We are both doing him a solid there."

"Good, I gave him your number he will call tonight and say he is a friend. He has your cell. Ham."

"As in the sandwich meat or Noah's son?" I asked.

He laughed. "Very good, Jimmy. The latter. I know child protection is important to you and this has that element to it."

I nodded.

He grasped my arm to get my attention. "It's bad. He needs help."

"He's got it," I said.

"How's your relationship with PD here?"

"On the Island?" I asked.

"Yes."

"Chief Mariano is a good friend. He was there when Mandy was killed. He personally took in my friend's two kids, before their grandmother got custody."

His face, although sad when I mentioned Mandy, broke into a big smile. "Mike Mariano," he said. "One of the best guys I ever had work for me. You can't find a man better than that."

I smiled. "Damned straight, Bern."

"Tell him I said hello and the when I'm done with this situation," he said referring to what he was working on that was all over the news. "The three of us will get dinner. If you're still friends with and Alex at Luger."

"I am, but you don't need me for that, pal. To date,

you're the only one I know of they ever started the ovens up for after they were turned off."

He smiled at the memory. He looked at his watch. As he did his driver rolled down the window and waved. He waved back. We shook hands and he walked toward his car.

"Oh, by the way," he said and turned around. "I work with a guy named Tony Shaffer."

"9-11 whistleblower. Great guy," I said.

"That's him. He may need you for something, so I gave him your info. Also a friend thing. Extend whatever courtesy you can but make money."

"Done."

I watched him drive off. I felt a little sad. I would never forget what he did for this city after the Towers came down. Then he was put in the shredder because politics demanded it. Sometimes I really did hate people.

I got back to the office and it was near suppertime. As I settled in, Grant called me. I could tell he was in a bad way and although the day had been tough I told him he was welcome to come in. I worked for a bit and then my stomach started to rumble. I remarked to the ceiling I was starving. Norina was still there and asked if I wanted anything from across the street. She was kind enough to order me some food.

He told me after I gave it to him he'd be here in about an hour. My cheeseburger and salad got there in ten and it was demolished long before they arrived. Norina left and I got more coffee for myself. It was after business hours when they arrived but we had recently hired a part time girl to work the phones for the building until eight and to help out with clients that came in to see us and the attorneys after hours. It would be rationale for a rent increase next year.

Hamilton Grant was about my height, give or take an inch. He was built heavy like me, but not like me. His traps were over developed, and he moved with a type of coiled energy only certain people had. His wrists and forearms were thick and I felt enormous strength in him when we shook hands. We were about the same age, I thought. His wife was tall maybe an inch taller than him. She was stunning. Long jet black hair that went past the middle of her back. Enchanting eyes. She reminded me of someone. I couldn't place it, but maybe we had met? The way she wore jeans would nominate the inventor of them for sainthood.

Ham introduced her to me as Sophia. He unconsciously pulled the client chair he sat in closer to hers. As he settled back in the chair, she reached for his hand and he took her hand and they sat like that, waiting for me to speak. She had the faintest hint of wearing good perfume. Grant's black hair was flecked with grey, and has hazel eyes were intense, obviously there was stress but he was also calm.

His wife had a small canvass brief case in her lap. Her free hand rested on it. I asked if I could get them coffee or something. They both politely declined. I liked them. Why were they so familiar? It hit me.

"Ham, you were a weightlifter?" By weightlifter I meant what most people refer to as Olympic style lifting.

He smiled and nodded. I had read an article about him a while back. That's why the overdeveloped traps. He threw some very impressive numbers up. There was speculation he and Shane Hammond might actually give the US a chance to place in the Olympics. But there was something else. I remembered.

"It was also you in the articles about that cult in Manhattan some years back."

"Yes." He smiled again but it was grimmer. "The Commissioner speaks highly of you," he said.

"He speaks well of you also."

There was something here. These were good people. I knew what he had done in the city. I felt it now. I don't know how to describe or not what level I perceived it. It was like there was a darkness enveloping them, surrounding them. I had this subconscious image of two lights, like the tribute they did at the Trade Center every year, the beams seemed to go into space. It was as if they were the light and the dark was crowding around them. I don't know how else to explain it but that mental image went as quickly as it came.

"How can I help you?"

"It's a long story, but I need you to look into something that happened, that is tied to me somehow. I need help in keeping my family safe."

"Whatever I can do, provided I can do it, you got," I said. "Tell me about it."

They looked at each other. A very sad expression was on her face and she squeezed his hand tighter. She smiled sadly at him and he squeezed her hand. She nodded and handed him the briefcase.

"It would be much easier if you read this and then we talked. It will take a while. I can leave it with you and a check. If you could arrange to meet me after or in the morning, it will tell you everything and we can answer any questions you might have."

"Okay," I said as my eyebrows raised. He opened the

briefcase and took out a manuscript, maybe a hundred pages. He handed it to me. It had no title.

He also took out a check book and asked me what my normal retainer was. I told him that as he was a friend of the commissioner's I could wait until I saw him tomorrow and asked him the questions. He shook his head.

"I'll need you, trust me. I need you personally to be involved. I spoke with the Commissioner. Tomorrow afternoon I'm meeting with the police again and I'd like you to be there, at our home. If you came a few hours earlier we could talk. I will need you. I am figuring based on what I know and have read about you, twenty-five thousand?"

I smiled. "That may be right, but I'll take ten from you, plus tax."

I told him who to make it out to, got the retainer agreement filled in, and we both signed it and I made him a copy. I saw the looks he and his wife exchanged. I put the manuscript he gave me on the center of my desk.

"Look, I can see this is something heavy. I don't know what I can do yet, but I'll help. If I can't you'll get your money back."

"Thank you," Sophia said. "I know this is unusual, but it will be easier this way. My husband has been through so much. It will be easier on him this way and probably save you some time."

"Good enough," I said.

"You see, my wife and..." He looked down a little. "A therapist that I've seen now and again, suggested that writing down what happened to me would help me deal with the trauma. My first lawyer, whom I am still in touch with, thought it was a good idea, too. He is very knowledgeable about these things."

"A law guardian?"

"Yes."

"And what happened to you as a child is part of this?"

"And what happened ten years ago," he said.

Sophia's eyes filled with tears. He noticed and he reached over and brushed them away from her eyes and ran his finger down her cheek.

"You are still in touch with your law guardian?"

"Yes."

I chuckled. They looked surprised. "I am sorry, I am not making light of this, of what happened to you. I am smiling because once again, it just goes to show how it is a small world after all. I see evidence of that all the time."

They both looked at me quizzically and I held my palm up asking them to wait. I walked over to the book case and took out "Strega" by Andrew Vachss. He had autographed it for me. I handed it to Ham.

"My God," he said. "How did you know?"

"It just made sense," I said. "Is he aware of what is going on now?"

"Not yet. I'm expecting his call tonight."

"Give him my regards," I said. "I will read this through and see you tomorrow. What time is the meeting with PD?"

"Four P.M.," Sophia answered.

"Who is supposed to be there?"

"The detectives handling the case and also one of their supervisors. A Chief. Chief Mariano." I smiled. "Do you know him?"

"Yes. Well. He is an exceptional man," I said. "So you know my retainer indicates that although you hire me I handle the case as I see fit."

"I understand and that's fine," Ham said. "I am in a similar business, and I do the same. I don't tell the doctor how to operate."

I nodded. "I will keep you in the loop," I told him. "If it became important in my opinion to let others know about what you wrote, how would you feel about that?"

He exhaled. "I'm not ashamed of anything in there. It's what happened. I may actually send it to a publishing house, I may not. I am torn about that. If anyone thought it was good enough, everyone will know about it. But it may help other..." He paused. "People in similar situations or maybe even some kids."

I gave both of them my cell number. I took theirs and their emails and home number. I saw them to the front door and gathered up what I needed and got ready to go. Cory texted me. I smiled. She had moved upstate a few months ago when she was accepted to a law school she applied to. It was my idea that we take a break. She was young. She had helped me through the worst part of my life to date. I didn't want her obligated. I told her it didn't have to be the end, take care of law school and we would stay in touch. She cried for hours. She told me she'd be faithful, I told her I knew she would. I told her I loved her but she was too young for this while she was going to law school and she needed to do that and make it *the* priority. If you think it was easy for me to do that, you couldn't be more wrong. Rhea and I had cautiously started seeing each other. She ended up having Rain and her daughter living with her. And man, was it complicated in my head. I loved

Cory, I was falling very quickly for Rhea and I would always love Mandy. I felt a twinge in my shoulder and I thought about Todd. And the creatures he worked for. I still thought about that fight with Todd. Hell on cold damp mornings it was like the bastard was in the room with me.

He ended up ratting the others out. He got a reduced sentence and gave them up. Evy got four years, Haskins ten and the Big G was in for seven. I don't know what they plead out to but while they weren't sweetheart deals as I'd call them they could have gotten much, much worse. There was a lot of money there and the lawyers and fixers they'd have would make the case hard. I was sad I didn't get to testify. So was Rain.

You will often hear prosecutors give this bullshit excuse that they want to save the victims from further trauma. No. I can tell you from personal experience, which was bullshit. Having a victim, even a kid, present in court, with the court officers, their lawyer and the judge and having them, even if they were children, get up, point at the garbage that abused them and say "they hurt me" would put them on the path to healing. Most of the time the prosecutor didn't want to take the chance of losing or the plea deal saved them a long trial. There were people that thought Law and Order was a documentary. They didn't know sometimes people were guilty of doing things like raping kids and there were no forensics. That just because the prosecutor said "he does the max" he had almost no power in whether or not that happened.

Rain and her Jewel were doing very well. Actually I thought of her now as *our* Jewel. Rhea was her family now. I was family to them also and they to me. I had

worried a little about us dating and Rhea had told me
no matter what nothing would change. I smiled and
told her so it could be even better with sex if it works
out. I had ducked when she swung at me but she didn't
really try. She was that rare person that meant it when
she said it. I'd throw myself in a shredder for all three of
them. Rhea had told me a few times Rain had woken up
crying. Sometimes she dreamed about the abuse and
sometimes she dreamt of me, fighting with Todd.

They had been watching an old movie with William
Smith and Rod Taylor called "Darker Than Amber." I
had recommended it to Rhea. One of the things I loved
about her was her love of crime fiction and noir. The
confrontation at the end was brutal and it was in some
ways similar to what she saw when Todd and I went at
it. She had left the room in a rush. I felt bad that hadn't
occurred to me. A friend of mine, Steve Browne, a liber-
tarian columnist from the mid-west, had suggested it to
me. The end confrontation between Taylor and Smith
was brutal and surprisingly realistic, for 1970. Turned
out when I looked it up it looked realistic because it was
real. Taylor and Smith both big strong guys, both had
been amateur boxers, went at it so the badly the crew
had to keep separating them. Smith had slipped and
broke Taylor's nose and Taylor had busted three of
Smith's ribs. It was also one of only two movies with the
venerable Travis McGee by John D. MacDonald and
was a good movie. She had called me at 2am the next
morning and we talked for an hour.

Vachss had slain the lawyers on the other side and
he got her and her daughter a settlement, ignored child
support, and gotten multiple times what he could have
gotten for that. And although you can't technically give

up visitation or support (well you could, but a quick trip to family court and that could change), with Vachss on her side that son of a bitch would never see that kid. I figured early on that the Big G's lawyers did not want Andrew Vachss questioning him in family court. It was one of the reasons when a family court case involving abuse was being heard in tandem with a criminal case, the prosecutors would ask for Vachss. No defense lawyer wanted him on the other side. Having him as the Law Guardian would result in no bad precedents and might result in the prosecutor getting some previously unknown info.

"Take that to the fucking bank," I said to myself as I smiled grimly.

I had come to love Mike Mariano like a brother. I was constantly soliciting him for when he retired. Jeff also thought it would be a great idea. He had not only been there for me when Mandy was killed, he made sure I was okay during the recovery from both the gunshot and the setbacks after going the distance with Todd.

He had Rhea and me over for dinner one night and I met his wife, and German Shepherds. On reflection it hit me that I was more fortunate than most when you consider the quality of the people I was fortunate to be close too. I also had more close friends than most.

I was almost home when Rhea called. I smiled when I saw the number. I was listening to Peter Frampton's live version of "Do You Feel Like We Feel." At this point, I'd interrupt "Stairway To Heaven" for her, and that was no small thing.

"Creed's male escort and ecstasy service, may I book your next appointment?" I asked.

She laughed. "As a matter of fact," she began. "I happen to be free tonight as Rain and the baby are going to a friend of hers and I declined joining them in favor of the possibility of seeing you."

"Then I could not possibly, in good conscience, not see you. Would you care to take a break from cooking? Rain told me you cooked for them almost every night. I can make something or we can order. I do have something I have to read tonight that is work related but it won't take that long and I would very much love to see you," I said.

"When?"

"Now. Yesterday."

"I'm free now. I'll see you soon."

"Any food preference?"

"Well as you have homework, let's order out and you can take me to bed right away."

"It's not just your kick ass body and your beautiful face, baby girl, I love the way you think the most."

I heard that magical laugh again and smiled. Denino's after all these years was finally delivering. We ordered a garbage pie, baked clams, salad and cannoli. I took her up on her offer and left warm beautiful woman and a warm comfortable bed to pay for the food. I didn't tell her I'd eaten earlier because I didn't want her to feel bad. And because I had no problem eating again. We'd eaten and she had a medical show on the discovery channel she liked on while I read Ham's book. She fell asleep with her head on my shoulder. She was wearing a flannel shirt I had and because she was tall it barely covered her, which met my approval. I had finished it and sat there making notes careful not to disturb her. I watched her face now and again while she slept and the beauty of her face helped me deal with the horror in the manuscript.

The cable box said it was not yet ten PM. I was able to get up and quietly went into the kitchen. I texted Mariano to see if he was awake. He responded by calling me.

"Hey, Jimmy, how are you?"

"I'm good, Chief. I have a new client. You and some of your detectives are meeting with him tomorrow afternoon. If you don't mind, I'd like to be there."

"Hamilton and Sophia Grant?" he asked.

"Yes."

"By all means be there."

"Great. Listen, there is something very wrong here."

"Based on what I know so far, no argument."

"It gets worse, Chief," I said. "He asked me to read a book he wrote about his life, to do that and question him after. I think you should read the book. I can scan it and email you as it's less than a hundred pages. There could be more things coming, and based on what I'm reading, it could be very bad."

"How bad?"

"You know, I assume, about him finding and saving the girl?"

"Yeah."

I took a deep breath. "Bad as in maybe some dead kids."

"Send the book."

I was able to scan it in just a few minutes because the pages weren't bound. I had an office model scanner/copier/printer in my home office in case of a work emergency. He had it by ten-thirty. He called me at midnight.

"Did you consider he might somehow be involved? In orchestrating it?" he asked me.

"I did, and I discarded it. He is the man in that book. Bernie Kerik vouches for him."

"Hey how is he?"

"He's doing great. Finally."

"Best PC we had during my career although it's kind of a tie with him and Bratton the first." He meant on Bill Bratton's second go round he caved in and was a crony of the worst mayor the city had ever had by all accounts. And he was still voted in twice.

"I told him when this was over we would meet at Luger for dinner."

"I'm there," he said. I heard another phone ring. "Hang on, Jimmy."

"This is Mike Mariano," I heard him say. He would have put the phone on mute if he didn't want me to hear. "That is not acceptable," he said. After another pause. "Okay maybe I threw you when I answered the phone. This is Chief Mariano and I want that file found. Now. When you find it, Sergeant, it is to be brought to me immediately. If it is tonight, and it should be, I want it brought to my house, directly. This is a priority, and if I don't get it the people responsible should be expecting transfers. To the ass end of the Bronx or whatever precinct is the furthest from where they live. Am I understood? Good."

"Hey, Jimmy, sorry about that," he said.

I put two and two together. "No problem, Chief. About the file from the incident in Manhattan with the cult?"

"Yes," he stated, a hint of irritation in his voice. "I'm going over our file on it as we speak, and I am not going to say "Speak of the Devil" with good damned reason. I'll brief you tomorrow and have a copy brought to the Grants. I was put here to keep crime down and I don't like what I'm reading here. These people hurt children. It is a miracle Ham isn't a goddamned serial killer. I'm sorry to have to put out the people in records who sleep most of the night but if I can 'd like to prevent them hurting more children," he said. "And both he and his wife are two special human beings. Adopting those kids and wanting to give them a better life."

"Unquestionably," I replied. We paused for a bit.

"So you came to the same conclusion I have," I said after a while.

"Yeah. Someone from Ham's past is involved. The symbol. I looked it up also. That is a unique combination of symbols and it isn't common I haven't found it anywhere else. I also requested the file on the initial case, where they found Ham, at his house. They arrested a number of people."

"I thought that was upstate?"

"It was and if they had it I could probably get it anyway but we were in on it for some reason. We will have our own file. I'll also interview our people involved in the incident ten years ago and get the names of whoever was involved on the first case back in the seventies. It's not likely they are still on the job, maybe dead but we will cross that bridge when we come to it."

"So this means at least with the girl on the road, and maybe with the incident across the street from the club, we likely have someone from Ham's past involved," I said.

"It can't be a coincidence. The prior detective, who did a good job and the feds when they got involved because of kiddie porn and child trafficking, checked him out. Nothing. But he is involved somehow."

"Agreed. But what do we have here? Someone meant for this to happen, the girl escaping just when Ham drove by? His wife, then his fiancée, just happened to see the kid getting dragged out of the car?"

"I don't know, Jimmy."

"If that is the case, someone has to be keeping tabs on him. Maybe someone close to him," I said.

"We need to explore that possibility," he said.

"According to his book he is cautious." I reflected. "There has to be a way someone is getting information," I said. "Has to be."

"Well, we'll find out soon enough," Mariano said.

"I'm going to see him early, but I'm going to hold off on heavy questions until you guys are there and let you take the lead."

Mariano knew me now. He knew I did my job well and I know what I'm doing. I also had to acknowledge it was PD that was investigation the crime. A girl had been kidnapped and assaulted. There might even be an attempted murder charge. I could help my clients without stepping on their toes and pissing them off. Although it was luck of the draw, you had a good chance of a seasoned NYPD detective making a difference, not to mention Mariano being involved. To say he knew what he was doing was like saying a politician knows how to lie.

Rhea appeared in the doorway to my office. She still had my flannel shirt on and black panties, she leaned on the door frame and blew me a kiss.

"Well, Chief, something else has come up that I

need to investigate before bed. If you need me give me a call, I'll keep the phone on."

"Oh yeah?" he asked. "What's her name?"

"I'll never tell," I said. I then went ahead with the new investigation.

Rhea and I had slept peacefully for a few hours when I woke at four thirty. I managed to get out of the bed without waking her. I spent a few hours researching Satanic Crimes on the internet and ordering a few kindle books.

12

WHEN IT WAS A REASONABLE HOUR, I called Jeff and asked him to cover for me, which was no easy feat. A lot was going on. He was happy about the check though and knew how important the case was. I called Ham and got his voicemail. I called Sophia and she told me that he was working out in the basement. I needed to do the same. I told her I'd like to come earlier, about ten o'clock. She said they would both be there.

I had offered to make breakfast for Rhea, but she had work early. Regrettably, I got the same response when I offered to have her for breakfast. I had a lot of trouble with the workout, which today was just bag work, heavy singles on trap bar deadlifts and grip work. I pulled five hundred easy. Five twenty-five decided not to cooperate. I decided not to do as heavy a warm up like bag work the next time. I did a half hour jog on the treadmill. When I was younger I had maxed out at 575 on this left and I wanted to do it again. Mariano and Ray Gordon, a good friend who had retired from the Navy as a SEAL after spending most of fifteen years in the Gulf, had convinced me, when Gordon had come up for a week a few months earlier and we were at Luger, to ditch the Glock .45 in favor of a Kimber .45 ACP. Ray had taught me how to shoot when I first got my license. The law which had been only seven round magazines ad been changed to ten before the touchy feely governor was ousted. I usually carried two extra magazines. I took three today.

While I cooled off before I showered, I threw some fruit in the blender with some protein powder and had two Portuguese rolls I'd bought a while back but had stored in the freezer. I thawed them and buttered them and had them with my coffee. The key was warm or room temperature roll and cold butter with hot coffee.

I regretted not having a third roll when I left. Grey sports jacket, dark blue oxford dress shirt and blue jeans. Ham didn't live far. Sophia made what was possibly the best coffee I'd ever had; at least it was in a close tie with the coffee Commissioner Kerik's wife, Hala, had once served me. When I'd told her that her husband belonged in the same club I did, men who were not really good looking enough to be with such a beautiful woman, she smiled and took my arm and said "Bernie I like him best of all your friends." Absolutely lovely woman and she shared the same quality that Sophia did, making you feel absolutely welcome in her home. I'd met Mark Owen at that occasion, the pseudonym that one of the SEALs who had written the book about killing Bin Laden, used.

Sophia also had pastries and the way she tended her kitchen along with her long black hair and the beauty of her face reminded me of Rhea. I punished myself for missing the five and a quarter dead lift by refusing the pastries. The first time she offered. Thirty seconds after the second time the plate was half empty. It turns out Sophia knew Rhea they both attended the same church, a Greek Orthodox Church. Ham eventually came down. I got up to shake hands with him and something on me popped. For a second I wondered if there was a problem but older dwellings tended to settle and shift.

"I remember when snap, crackle, and pop was the sound my cereal made and not what I heard getting out of a chair," I said. Sophia gave a nice genuine laugh and Ham smiled.

"Tell me about it," Ham said.

He sat at the table after he made coffee for himself and Sophia. She had one into the other room to make sure things were okay with the kids as they got ready for school.

"We need to consider the possibility," I started, "that this does have something to do with your past. If you pushed me on it, I'd say it has to. In that case we may want to take precautions with your kids."

Sophia looked alarmed. Ham nodded. "Are my kids in danger?" she asked me.

"I don't know but we have to consider that possibility. If you are asking me as a security professional," I began.

"Then you have to take the possibility of the threat very seriously," Ham finished for me. I nodded. "My kids have been home to be safe. They missed the last few days of school."

"I want my kids safe, Jimmy," Sophia said earnestly.

"What are they doing today?" I asked.

They told me the kids were going to class, Elias to college and Stephanie to high school.

"Maybe we should make a decision then," I told them. "How are they doing in school?"

"They are both doing very well."

"Would it hurt them to take more time off?"

"They may not want to, but if you think it's important," Sophia began.

"You have to make a decision. Do you want safety to be paramount, or—"

Sophia interrupted me. "Yes," she said emphatically.

"Then tell them to take off until we can figure out what the hell is going on."

"I'll tell them," Ham said.

Their kids made their way into the kitchen. The son a lean but powerful looking kid, had worked out with his father, Sophia mentioned to me. They were polite and they both shook hands with me when their father told them I'd be working with them, as a precaution. The boy was apparently of driving age as he was supposed to have been dropping his sister off and then driving to the college he attended. Ham took them down what I figured was the basement stairs.

"How is that going to go?" I asked Sophia.

"Ham loves our children. He is good to them. But he also raises them right. He will tell them they aren't going, then he will tell them why. They know about what happened to him and they have been going to therapy themselves for years. We have given them more freedom as time goes on and they have acted responsibly. As soon as we felt they were old enough, we took them to the shooting range and he paid for a class on gun safety. He had the instructor explain to them how serious firearms were. We made them understand the consequences of pulling a trigger."

"So it was no longer the mysterious forbidden fruit," I said.

"Yes. They also know not to talk about them or tell people we have them."

I nodded approvingly. "How bad was what happened to them?" I asked her.

"We aren't exactly sure. They were young he was eight and she was six. They were the children of two of the cult members but they weren't tortured like Ham was. They were emotionally and psychologically abused, but their lives were normal on the outside. And it looks like the night that we found them would have been the first time that they," she went quiet and her eyes looked down.

"Were going to be sexually abused?" I asked her and simultaneously finished what she was saying.

She nodded.

Ham came back and Sophia gave him another cup of coffee, a man and a woman after my own heart. Consuming or providing coffee said much about the true nature of someone's soul.

"Guys, although I want to hold off on the heavy duty inquires until PD gets here, I want to ask a few things," I said. "I spoke with Chief Mariano last night. He is taking a personal interest in this case. He understands that this could lead to someone hurting children and he doesn't want that. He read your book as well Ham."

"Did he have anything to say of interest?" Sophia asked.

"Well like me, he thinks you are both amazing people."

Sophia smiled and blushed a little. Ham did smile

but it was fleeting. His countenance was serious he had a question but he was going to wait for me to finish.

"He also has the same feeling that Ham is somehow connected to this. It cannot be a coincidence. He had ordered the file from the incident ten years ago to be brought to him and I believe if the detectives that investigated it are still on the force, they will be seeing him. He also said that NYPD had something to do with the original situation with Ham way back, even though it was upstate."

"I remember telling Walt, the cop that rescued me that my brother had brought me a picture of the Empire State Building. But I don't remember much. I know they all tried hard to find my brother, that there was a man that had something to do with the monster that called himself my father. I have a vague recollection of what he looked like. My brother spent a lot of time with him. They could never figure out who he was. After the night in Manhattan, NYPD and the Feds tried to find them again. As far as the incident ten years ago, the detectives worked the hell out of that case. There was a lot pf pressure on them. They were good people. They knew there had to be a connection to my past. They looked. Hard. They went upstate reviewed the prior investigation from when I was rescued, they tracked down Walt, the cop who rescued me. They came to see me at least fifteen times. The cult members all went to prison. Somebody pulled some strings and they were no slap on the wrist sentences. The prosecutor in charge wasn't having it. All of the cult members were into kiddie porn no one got less than twenty years, except for two of them that ratted on everyone else. They got eighteen years."

I smiled and shook my head. "Was the prosecutor," I started to ask.

Ham nodded. "Alice Vachss."

"God damn," I said. "Boy did they get what they deserved. A Vachss to the left of them, A Vachss to the right of them."

"She is one tough lady," Sophia said.

"Hell yeah," I said. "You couldn't get a better prosecutor than that."

Ham downed the rest of his coffee. As he sat there talking Sophia had put her hand on his shoulder and he reached across and held her hand. They really were something to see. There is a lot of pain there and they bore it well. They took those kids in and made them family and it was obvious as strong as he was Ham leaned on her. That kind of pain would have broken most people, killed most relationships. She had to be an amazing woman.

"It kind of snowballed after," Ham continued. "The cops got warrants and raided the homes of all the cult members." His voice was bitter. "Cult members." He scoffed. "For the most part, freaks that get off on hurting kids and make money by filming themselves hurting kids. A lot of people went down for it. But they never found the leader. And one other thing," he said as he looked at me.

"The human garbage that was raising our children. They weren't their biological children. They refused to say how they got them."

That hit me as strange. "So safe to say they weren't the rats."

"Yeah," Ham said, nodding. "They both got thirty years."

Although Sophia was visibly worried to have her fears confirmed or at least the possibly supported, she seemed relieved also. Ham was still serious. Stoic might be a better description.

"Does he think I might be involved? In a bad way? Maybe because of the trauma and abuse?"

I shook my head. "No. We did discuss that briefly but we both agreed you knowingly have no part in this. But we also agree that you are likely some kind of target. Besides, it doesn't at all seem plausible to me, on top of everything else, that you'd have been involved if Alice Vachss was the lead and she didn't uncover it. Andrew would also have known. The freaks don't have a camouflage that would work on him. If something had gone wrong with your wiring and he kept in contact with you, he'd have known," I said.

He nodded. "He was happy that you were involved in the case. He did ask me to ask you one thing, though."

I raised my eyebrows. "He wanted to know if you had been incorporating peek-a-boo? Or that you were at least working on your ducking and slipping? He said you'd know what he meant."

I burst out laughing. Ham and Sophia looked at each other and smiled then looked back at me questioningly.

"I had a confrontation with someone and I managed to prevail, barely, and I took some lumps."

"I remember!" Sophia exclaimed as we looked at her. "Ham, remember that picture of him in the paper, you said to me I'd hate to see what the other guy looked like."

"Oh yeah!" Ham said, laughing. "I heard about that, it must have been one hell of a fight."

"It was and I hadn't quite recovered from being shot. He was tough."

Memories flooded in. "And when I saw Andrew, he said "Oh, Jimmy" You maybe want to work on ducking and slipping more." I had two black eyes and a busted nose at the time. I laughed like crazy and my cracked ribs screamed at me for that. Sophia poured me more coffee.

"Temporary measures aside, whatever else you do, Jimmy," Sophia said. "I want my kids to be safe."

"Upon assessing the situation and the risk, count on it," I said. "And take whatever recommendations we make seriously."

"You, can count on that," Ham stated.

I nodded. "Are most of your people that were with you that night in the city, still with you? If we need to talk with them?"

"Yes, almost all of them. As a matter of fact, we are getting together Sunday morning. We train the guys two or three times a month at a martial arts school here on the island."

I laughed. "At House of Karate, in Great Kills?"

Ham's eyebrows raised.

"I know Smitty he was my teacher. He has done that for a number of Nightclubs, given them space and even worked with their staff on removing people without getting sued for it. He told me about you guys using his school."

"Great guy," Ham said. "Very tough. He ran a few clubs for me in the nineties and early two thousands."

"I just saw him not long ago because he knocked some dope out at a Dunkin Donuts."

"Even though he has to be up there in years, I don't doubt that," Ham said.

"Some idiot was knocking his girlfriend around and he took exception," I said.

"That's him," Ham said with a laugh. He suddenly looked worried.

"Nothing to indicate that but we can't discount the possibility," I said.

"He should know, it may be important," Sophia said softly. Ham nodded. I waited.

"Smitty's son Ken, the doctor, do you know him?"

"Like my brother. Good man, like his dad."

Ham nodded. "The other little boy, the one they cut on that goddamned altar," Ham said. "Ken was the doctor treating him, making the scar as diminished as possible. Those bastards killed the kid's mother in front of him. Ken ended up adopting him. He and my son are good friends."

Okay the small world stuff just exploded. I shook my head. I knew Ken had adopted his son. I instantly knew it made sense for Ken not to have talked about what happened to the boy.

"Could the boy and Ken's family be in danger?" Ham asked me.

"Possibly. We will let them know what's going on."

"I already called him and told him Kerik had recommended you. He thought that was funny because he would have recommended you also," Ham said. "Well, funny is the wrong word. A coincidence would be better."

"The same way Commissioner Kerik helped us adopt the kids, he got Ken to help with his son Sam. He knew Kenny from Ground Zero and felt he would be able to help the boy with removing or at least making the scar less prominent. Kenny came to love the boy and adopted him.

Ken was one of the most highly regarded Cosmetic Surgeons in the country. He was an absolutely brilliant doctor. He started off as a cancer surgeon at Sloan. He then moved on to cardiac surgery, was very skilled but didn't find it challenging enough. Eventually he settled on Trauma surgery. Despite being in Philadelphia he ended up being one of the first medical responders on 9-1, having left for New York when the first plane hit. He'd gone to Haiti after the Earthquake and spent a few weeks amputating limbs on top of cars. Before that and after his time at ground zero he no longer wanted to be the last person someone saw before meeting the reaper. He threw himself into Cosmetic Surgery, and was highly skilled at it. He also was my personal doctor and kept himself in the loop both when I got shot and had the throw down with Todd. We were talking about getting a pool going to see when arthritis would make itself known in various places on me.

"We all felt that as at least the leader got away, the kids might still be in danger. No one knows our kids or Ken's son were the kids from that night. We thought it was safer."

"You thought right," I said.

I smiled thinking of my friend. That was him. That was what the man I knew would do. Smitty talked about his grandkids all the time and Sam was no exception. I'd met him at several occasions. Kids could be resilient. There is no exact understanding why some kids that endured abuse would become monsters but others, most wouldn't, although many of those would go on to hurt themselves. I personally thought it had something to do with the kids coming under the influence of good people, people that loved them, after the trauma. If it ever was fully figured out, it would be like finding the Rosetta Stone for child abuse.

"Maybe that assessment should be the priority?" Ham asked me. The concern was evident on his face.

"Exactly what I was thinking. Part of that assessment," I said, "is figuring out what the hell the connection is to you."

Their doorbell rang. "Expecting someone?" I asked.

"My friend, a business associate who runs most of the clubs I have and a few of my security people. We have a few things to go over. They were all there that night."

Three men and one woman followed Sophia into the kitchen. The first man, who looked to be lean and in very good shape was introduced to me as Foster. The next two guys were about the same height maybe five eleven and weight. Three maybe three hundred and twenty pounds of muscle that appeared to be carved from granite. The black man was introduced to me as Dwayne and the white man as Carl. The woman's name was Vivian. She was very pretty, red hair also in shape. Foster and Vivian were both carrying. Although Vivian was very attractive what you first noticed about her was that hardness cops have after years on the job.

We sat at the large kitchen table and talked a bit. Sophia served all of them although once in a while someone would get up like Vivian did and get cream out the fridge for her second cup of coffee. They were all comfortable here. There was obviously great affection, a family affection between all of them. At one point, Ham had to get up and take a phone call.

"If there's anything we can do," Foster said to me. "Name it."

"How about you all text me your numbers, name, and Ham after your name so it's easy to find you."

They all did. I asked them to tell me about Ham how they knew him and there were some amusing stories there. I was generally just trying to get an impression of them. They were good people. I liked them. Having a great crew myself, I could appreciate them. I had no doubt they worked together well. It turned out that Foster had shot one of the freaks the night they broke in on the ceremony.

"Were you okay after?"

"I spent years, active, in the military," he told me. His voice was unusual in that there was no detectable accent. At least I couldn't detect it. He spoke clearly and used proper language. "SBS, I spent a good deal of time in the middle east. It wasn't my first time."

I nodded. Foster didn't really have an English accent although he pronounced every word correctly. He spoke softly and forcefully at the same time.

"None of us are strangers to violence," Carl said. Dwayne is a captain in the FDNY, and he worked and grew up in some hard places. Vivian is a second-grade detective, and I've been working the door at bars since I was sixteen. But what we saw that night. I never saw anything like it, nothing like it since."

"I hope I never see anything like it again," Dwayne said. He shook his head. "How could they do that to kids? I still ask that question."

"Yeah, me, too," I said. "We are the only species that allows predators to prey on our young, a good friend has said."

"That's accurate," Vivian said.

"They do it because they like doing it," Foster said quietly.

"Yeah," I said, agreeing with Foster.

I looked at my watch and saw I still had a few hours before I met PD here. I had made an appointment to get my hair cut. My friend Melissa owned a Salon called Golden Touch on Watchogue Road. Bobby Bianchi would chastise me for not getting my hair cut at his top-of-the-line Salon, although I frequently gave his gift certificates out for massages etc. But as I told him, I wanted a haircut that I didn't need to take a second mortgage out on my house to pay for.

The alarm on my phone went off. Despite my luddite leaning mentality, I had to admit this damned phone replaced a lot of equipment, and it fit in my pocket.

I had a lunch scheduled tomorrow on Long Island with Nick Giordano. We had become friends after he scheduled me on The P.A.S. Report, his podcast to discuss the rapid rise in violent crime. He was a college professor and had garnered considerable attention when he discovered the majority of his students couldn't discern between U.S. and Russian Constitutions.

Using the aforementioned tool of societal deconstruction, I sent him a quick email asking for a rain check.

I then called Ken Testa, who—as it turns out—would be in surgery for another forty-five minutes or so.

My pharmacy was across the street from Ken's office, so I decided to kill two birds with one stone there as well. I wondered why the PIs in movies and TV didn't have to do things like get prescriptions or go shopping. I rubbed my shoulder, which twinged on cue. They also recovered from being shot a hell of a lot faster.

I took the quick ride over to Golden Touch where I surprised Melissa by both remembering my appointment and showing up on time. I'd taken my e-reader with me, so I read up on Satanic Crimes while I waited the fifteen minutes for her to be free.

Considering what she had to work with, she did her usual bang up job, and I was in and out.

I stopped off on the way to Ken's at my favorite Hot Dog Truck. My friend Dawn operated "Skippy's" Hot Dog Truck on Hylan Boulevard. It had been in her family for years. She had not as of yet heeded my advocacy for Hot Pretzels as well, so I satisfied myself with 3 dogs, loaded with kraut and mustard, and a seltzer. Properly fed and groomed, I headed off to see Doc.

13

I PARKED in Ken's parking lot and went across the street first to the Pharmacy. Even though the pharmacy was across the island from me I picked up my prescriptions there. I had gone to a chain and after the cuddle fest with the Toddster. I went there to fill a prescription for pain meds. Initially they held up on filling it and I got a lecture from the pharmacist about the dangers of meds and he started asking me question to see if I had a problem with the pills. I informed him that I didn't need him, or anyone else to insert themselves between my doctor and myself. I may have been in a bad mood to start, the multitude of injuries and trying to breathe through my broken nose competing for my attention sort of ensured that, but being spoken to like I was a societal scourge didn't elicit kindness from me.

"Do you think I broke my own nose, got these two black eyes because I thought I'd look sympathetic? Would you like to see the bruises where my ribs are cracked? How about the scar from my shoulder surgery where I had been shot and there were fresh bruises? How about the scar on my knee where I had arthroscopy last week? Or a whole bunch of other injuries, would you like me to strip?"

The problem is there was abuse of prescription pain medication. But there were also people who needed it. If you went back twenty years, many people that needed them, who were suffering couldn't get them. Vachss had written a book that in addition to child protection focused on this. It was called Pain Management. That's how the government was. A pendulum swing. No one could get it. Then people were getting it for hang nails. The truth was always somewhere in the middle, but the government was all or none.

It occurred to me at that moment I didn't do enough to help support small businesses and I got the doctor's office on the phone and had the script transferred.

When I walked back across the street Fran, Ken's office manager, was in the parking lot and greeted me with the over-abundance of cheer she always had. She could make the sun come out when it was raining. She was a kind woman, and looked at least twenty years younger than she was.

"I thought that was your car!" she said as she kissed me on the cheek, gave me a hug and ushered me in.

Ken was in a consult so she brought me to the kitchen and made us both coffee and we sat and talked a while until Ken finished up. Like the office mother she actually was, after Ken greeted me with a quick hug and sat down, she made him coffee as well.

"How is your dad?" I asked.

"No more parking lot knock outs so far," he said.

"That you know of," I replied.

I had gone to see Smitty after Ken had called me and told me about the altercation he had in the Dunkin Donuts parking lot. "You have to talk to my dad, Jimmy, he has a heart condition he can't keep doing this, we'll lose him. He'll listen to you."

When he opened the door I was greeted with "Did my son send ya?"

I told him he was the rock for his family and so many others. And I told him we all needed him to be around for a while longer. He was quiet and as we sat on his front steps he looked at me.

"Jimmy, when I walked in to get my wife and me coffee and donuts this bastard was cursing at the girl, she was cowering. Stuff no one should say to a woman. I don't need to tell you, I raised you."

I nodded.

"When I came out he cracked her one and knocked her off her feet. I put the stuff down and looked at him and told him if he wasn't such a cowardly piece of shit maybe he'd try that on me. I still move well enough, I put him down one shot."

"You got a heart condition, Sensei."

"Jimmy, I want to die as me. One day it'll be my time and I want to go out as me, the way I lived. Besides, my father's last knockout came when he was eighty-three. I want to tie that record." He had just turned eighty.

I went to see Ken and told him I loved his dad, too, but he can't change who he is at this point. Kenny sadly agreed. There were very few men like him left.

"Everything okay?" Ken asked me.

"Actually, Doc, I need to talk to you," I said.

"That's my cue," Fran said. She smiled and got up and went back to her office.

"Talk to me."

"I've been hired by Hamilton Grant. Someone may be stalking him or his kids and that someone has something to do with his past. He told me about Sam. Out of concern. Whatever is going on has some link to his past and it may extend to his kids. It may extend to Sam."

"Jesus Christ," he said.

"I just for now want you to keep your eyes open, I will figure this out sooner or later."

"What brought this about?"

I told him about Ham almost running over the girl running from whomever had kidnapped her. I told him about the symbol. He understood right away. Although he was staring at a worker's comp notice that hung on the wall and didn't say anything for a while, he had one somewhere else. It was a while before he got back.

"He was supposed to stay with us temporarily. Kerik knew me from Ground Zero. I actually helped a friend of his out with a scar issue. We were talking about having kids, adopting, fostering, all of it. We had been approved as foster parents. He told me they killed Sam's mom, stabbed her to death in front of him. They were then carving a fucking star into his chest. Bastards. He was such sweet little boy. He trusted me right off the bat. He let me work on his scar and one day when I was doing that he asked if I could be his real dad. It broke my heart. I called Kerik, he said he'd help, we hired a lawyer and Sam became our son."

We were both quiet a while. The gravity of what had been and what might be hung on both of us. The phone rang and Fran had called over the intercom who it was and Ken had asked her to please tell them he would call back. He responded yes when she asked if she should hold his calls. "Unless it's an emergency," he added.

"Jimmy, he still has nightmares about what happened. He still goes to therapy. He's always afraid someone will come and take him or take us from him. Except for Ham's kids he has very few friends. I'm worried about what will happen to him if I tell him. Do you think I need to? Should I hire security? What should I do?"

"Doc, I needed to let you know about the possibility. I honestly don't know what the actual threat level is but this has to have something to do with Ham's past. It can't be a coincidence. Keep him close for a bit, tell your dad, whoever else you need to. I know it may upset him but God Forbid there is a risk and we do nothing. I will help and do whatever you might need. I'll call you after the meeting this afternoon."

"Okay," he said. "I hope I didn't offend you by not telling you about all this before."

I held my hand up. "Stop. You did right. The idea was to be on the safe side."

"Thank you."

"He in school today?"

"Yeah, I'm picking him up."

"Okay, do that and we will talk later." I got up to leave and the phone rang. Ken gave me a quick hug and before I could go Fran came in.

She looked at both of us concerned. "Doc. Nicky from the pharmacy across the street is on the phone. He wants to talk to you or Jimmy, he said he thinks it might be important."

Ken and I looked at each other. He shrugged and said "Go ahead, Jimmy."

"Hey, Nick, everything okay?" I asked.

"Jimmy I saw this guy pull up about five minutes after you did, he's parked in the restaurant parking lot. There are two guys in the car and they are staring at Doc's office. I went over to get a menu to order lunch and they ducked down real fast."

"Did you happen to get the plate or can you tell me the type of car?"

Ken was staring intently. I wrote down the plate and make of the car a relatively new black Chevy Malibu. It was a Georgia license plate.

"It could be a rental car or it could be someone from Georgia." Or probably a half dozen other possibilities, I thought.

"Two guys, both in their 40s, average height and weight but hard to be certain because they were sitting. One had a beard the other clean shaven both had dark hair. One wearing a flannel shirt the other a light black leather jacket."

"Not bad, Nick, for a pharmacist."

"Hey, I listen to those stories you tell."

"Yeah, you only fell asleep once," I said. He laughed. "Thanks, pal. I'll let you know if anything comes of it, thanks for keeping an eye out."

I called my office and got Norina. I gave her the plate told her to run it, if it came back to a man in his forties, run his driver's abstract. Then hit it with the full barrage of database searches, first on whoever it was, then all the people at the address, businesses at the address see who had a record that lived there. "Go all out, and please I know it's a pain email or text me the information as it comes back most important is the DMVs, and the follow ups ASAP."

"Everything okay, Jimmy?" she asked me.

"I honestly don't know. It could be nothing. Speaking of which, if it does turn out to be nothing I'll call you or send you a message that reads abort so that we aren't blowing coin. I don't know if this is connected to an actual case or not."

She told me she understood and hung up.

Fran, Ken, and I looked at each other. Ken told Fran to keep an eye on the front door he and I checked the camera system I had installed for him and we could see the car sitting on the monitor. In just a few seconds I went back and saw the car pull into to the lot and then it moved so that whoever was driving had a better view of Ken's office.

"Could this be anything on your end, Doc?"

"Not that I'm aware of. I can't think of anything in my life where I'd have someone watching me."

"What about a disgruntled patient, maybe called in a complaint, a lie about something?" I knew Ken, you could eat off the floors and you had better odds on hitting lotto than you did him not following rules or regs. It didn't make sense they were there for me? They got there five minutes after I did. If they were following me, it wouldn't have taken that long? Or did Nick misjudge the time?

I stared at the wall. I ran things through my mind and tried to clear away the refuse. Once in a while when I was trying to figure something, I'd zone out. How were they keeping tabs on Ham? He had his house swept. Out of habit I check my rearview mirror often. It's possible they could have tailed me but I didn't think so. Maybe it's nothing, maybe it was happenstance.

"Jimmy?" I had the impression Ken had called my name more than once.

"How about this, Doc. I'll leave first and if they follow me we will know they were here for me. Unless," I said with a half-finished thought.

"Unless?" Ken asked me.

"Unless they did follow me to you, unless it does have something to do with Ham and by extension your son."

"Jesus Christ Jimmy," he began.

"Look, Doc, it would be one hell of a thing if they pulled that off. I went to Ham's home this morning. How would they know? Ham or Sophia wouldn't call someone and tell them. They kept what they knew about you quiet, all these years and only told me now because they were afraid for you. How the hell would someone find out that fast? The guy actually has his house swept, so it's not like there would be a bug at his house and Jesus you know what's involved with something like that? Not only that I check my rearview mirror also. I didn't make a tail. We don't even know yet if it is connected. And if it is connected then it's a good thing that we found out."

"You're right, Jimmy. It's just, I'm afraid for my son, after everything he went through. It still hovers over him like a black cloud."

I put my hand on his shoulder. "I know Doc. I give you my word, I will do whatever I can to help you and your family."

He smiled. "That I already know, Jimmy."

"I'll leave, and you watch the cameras. If they follow

me then I'll find out who they are. If they don't, I'll pull down the block and wait for you to leave. If they pass you, I'll follow them and we'll talk on the phone and plan the next move. Give me five. I want to call Jeff and let him know what's going on."

I got in my car without looking at the Chevy. I rolled the windows down. I hadn't heard the Chevy start and there's a good chance I would have as there wasn't a lot of activity or noise in the neighborhood. I called Jeff and updated him. I could hear the concern in his voice.

"Jimmy, be careful, okay?"

I knew what he was thinking because I was thinking it. We were both thinking about Bertone and Sullivan parked near our office to follow Mandy.

"Count on it, Papa Bear. Listen I need something else, who is around? I need someone to go over to Doc's house and see if there happens to be a tail set up."

"I can go."

"That'd work," I said giving him the address. "Two more things, call the Chief, let him know this may have a tie in and we may need him if this turns out to be the actual bad guys."

"Got it. The other thing?"

"Didn't you say Ray Gordon was up and in Atlantic City?"

"Yes, he is visiting family and taking a few days off to stay at The Borgata."

I chuckled. "Tell that libertine that I need him, life or death and we guarantee him his rate of pay for at least three days."

"Normally I'd worry about expenses here kid but if you need *HIM* I'll feel better if he is here keeping an eye on you." We hung up.

Ray Gordon and I have done a good bit of work together over the years. He was a very good, meticulous investigator but it would also be good to have him around, if things started to go bad.

I ran through everything in my head again, you always miss something but considering we didn't even know if we had something here, it looked pretty well covered to me.

I took my time pulling out, put my left signal on and waited till no cars were visible on the street in either direction. I pulled out slowly and made the left turn. No tail. Hell maybe they had nothing to do with me. I called Ken and told him. I situated myself in front of a dumpster that had been dropped in front of a house that appeared to be undergoing renovation. I backed in and it looked like there was no way they'd see me when they passed unless they specifically looked at me. I let my seat go back anyway.

"Okay Doc, I'm in position."

He kept the phone on. I could hear him getting in his Land Rover. I heard the door close and the engine start. He actually had the Land Rover so that no matter what the weather, he could get to a patient if they needed him.

"Making the left Jimmy, how far down are you?"

"I'm parked just after the big red dumpster, Doc. I..."

"They're on me, Jimmy."

"Copy, Doc. I'll be on them." Doc passed and they passed right after. They were right behind him. I gave it a few seconds and pulled out.

"Keep it slow and steady, Doc. They are either amateurs because they are right behind you or they are going to make some kind of move on you. Leave a space between you and any car in front of you. If you see one of them get out of their car, book it. Copy?"

"Yes, I understand," my friend said.

"By the way, Doc. I don't actually know what that means."

"What's that, Jimmy?"

"Copy. I have no idea what it means. All these military and ex-cop guys and gals that work for me, they always say "Copy" and I have no idea what it actually means. I'm just winging it."

He got a good laugh out of that, and knowing my friend, it helped keep him centered.

"If you have to do any wet work, I'll double your usual fee," he said.

"Considering my usual fee for you is zero, triple it. I'm worth it."

"Done."

"Doc, seriously, if they make a move on you, get out. I'll intercede. It looks like they are the only car. Always the chance they are in contact with another car, but gauging by how quickly they jumped on you, I'd say probably not."

"Okay. I'm coming up to the light on Hylan."

"I see. I'm behind that black four by four behind them. Remember, keep a space in front of you in case you have to get out."

Did they follow me to him or did they just happen to arrive after I got there? We decided as he drove that he would head in the general direction of the college. Wagner College and St John were both within blocks of each other. His son was in Wagner, where Ham's son Elias went. If they were still with him at that point, he would go to St. John's and we would have the option of misdirection. While I sat at the light, Jeff texted me the car was a rental.

"Jimmy should we call the cops?"

"I had my partner let Chief Mariano know Doc, but they haven't done anything yet. Besides this might be a chance to find out what the hell is going on."

"I just wish it wasn't happening where my son is at risk."

"Risk is minimal Doc, I doubt they are going to try to take him at the school and if we don't like the way it looks, you go in the school, they have security right there and you don't budge, the cops will be on the way. This way here we are in control. If it turns out to be nothing he never has to know."

I noticed that a car was behind me and the two guys in the front were somewhat animated. One of them kept looking over his shoulder. One of them pointed ahead. The light turned and Ken moved. The driver in the car behind me had turned to say something over his shoulder and the passenger tapped him on the shoulder and pointed. Only Ken had moved. It came together quick. There were two cars. One of them sat in the parking lot for Italianissimo and had eyes on Ken's car. The car behind me was likely in communication by phone or radio. They were probably supposed to call the car behind me and it would take the lead. For some reason maybe the second car wasn't in position and the car in the lot had to take the lead.

I wasn't taking any chances now. I told Ken to call the school and ask for security to get his kid and bring him to the security office and to stay on the phone until he was brought there. I called Jeff and told him to call the Chief and tell him someone was likely moving on

Doc or his kid. I told him to call Smitty who would probably be at his school at this time of day and tell him what was going on. I was going to have Ken go to the pizza place down the block from Smitty's school. There was an alley next to it, and I had a plan.

Doc called me back. The kid had been taking a class in the same building where the security office was. The guy that ran security there was an ex-cop. Ken told him what was happening that there may be an attempt to kidnap his son. The guy told him the kid would stay safe with them.

"Doc, head to the Village Maria. Grab a table there and wait for instructions, we have back up on the way, they did have a second car. We have re enforcements coming. Take the sea there, do not look around, order a slice play with your phone but don't eyeball these guys. Keep the same carefree demeanor on you at all times. We don't want to spook these guys, but I want to know what the hell is going on."

I paused at this moment to give silent thanks to all of the politicians on Staten Island who had profited from the over building and population increase which ensured at least a half hour ride to get 7 miles at this time of day. The phone beeped to let me know someone else was calling in.

"Doc that's the Chief, head to the Pizza Place remember I'm behind you, your dad knows it's all good."

"Okay, Jimmy. If these guys are here for my kid, then I am going to need to chat with them."

Ken had been a trauma surgeon. He didn't ask any questions. He was probably cooler than I was. "I will try to arrange that doc talk in a bit."

"Chief!" I said. "How you be?"

"Hi, Jimmy. I understand you've been poking the bear."

"Of course," I said. "And wearing a meat vest while I'm doing it."

"I wouldn't expect any less. What have we got?"

"First, I think we need some help at the Village Maria Pizzeria."

"I'm a few minutes away. I have two cars two blocks away. Jeff filled me in while I started making my way there. I was going to the precinct and then we were going to the meeting at your client's home."

He lived about five minutes from the precinct where his office was and that was closer to the pizza place than we were. The thing about Mike was he was a leader. He had the balls to be the first guy through the door, but the brains to know when it was the right time to go through that door. He couldn't have gotten the whole story.

"Chief, I don't know what the hell is going on, but the way I read it these guys were following Doc to get to his kid. He was the kid that those the freaks were carving the pentagram into, when Ham and his guys broke in on the cult ten years ago. Jeff has extra security at Ham's place and they will wait on us. He has two of the biggest guys I've ever seen in my life that work for him there, two other people armed, ex-detective named Vivian Potter, as well as the manager of the club, who is also armed. This is a shortcut, I think, to finding out what the fuck is going on."

"I read the files, Jimmy, and I spoke to the lead detective, Bill Sebastian. I know him. These people hurt kids. For the most part, whoever it is in charge, he's a true believer. The rest of them, they're just freaks that get off on hurting kids and filming it. I am all for a short-cut. They kidnapped that girl the other night. They are now in my borough and I want it stopped."

We planned out what to do. The black four by four stayed behind me. Ken drove leisurely, we'd be there in five minutes. I hung up with the Chief as Doc was calling in.

"My father is there," he said.

"If I recall right the guy that owns the place, he is a student of your dad's right?"

"Yeah, him and his wife and kids, the whole family."

"Tell your dad he has five minutes to get as many people out of there as he can. Tell him the Chief will be there and probably some of his cops."

"Call you right back."

We were only blocks away now and my heart rate was increasing. I took a deep breath to steady it and let it out slow and controlled. The phone rang again sixty seconds later.

"He said it's a little slow anyway, he is in there, he met Chief Mariano a few times when he was visiting shops in the community, and Chief Mariano is standing across the street. He brought this kid Joe with him. He's a cop but he has a baby face. Okay I'll make the right after I pass the Pizzeria and park and go in."

"Copy Doc, I'll park around the corner. They've seen me so I'll go to your table." I was about to hang up and it hit me. "Doc, grab that kid Joe and pretend he is Sam, call your dad and let him know we are doing that."

"You got it."

I saw him make the right at the light. The Pizzeria was on the corner. The car following him made the right as well. Ken parked. I stopped to make a left at the light. The black four by four behind, me looked like it was going straight and for a second my gut dropped. If I misread all this, I was in for it. A half second later they made the right but it was along half second. Oncoming traffic stopped me from making the turn but it gave me a few seconds to watch. Three guys got out of the Four by Four. Big guys. The biggest about six two well over two fifty. The other two built the same way and about six foot each. I parked my car and found Mariano watching through the gap between two cars parked at the meters across the street from the Pizzeria.

I had gotten to know him over time. So it wasn't strange to me that and NYPD Chief was standing here with me, ready to go hands on. I'd have been surprised before I met him.

I slid in next to him. "Damn this neighborhood is going downhill in a hurry," he said, keeping his eyes on the situation across the street.

"Are you casting aspersions upon me, Wereowance?"

"Is that English?"

"Native American. For Chief."

"And you speak some of the Native languages?"

"I read it in a Nero Wolf novel. I'm culturally appropriating the word."

"Well you can't be locked up for that. Yet." He mused. "For a guy with a twenty-inch neck, I must say, you read a lot. Now if you could just stop moving your lips when you read."

"That hurts, Chief."

"You'll live," he said with a chuckle.

"What have we got?" I asked.

"I got three cars around the corner. They'll run if

they see uniforms and squad cars or at the least not do anything. Plan clothes people are close, be here in a few minutes. I want to get something that proves these people are at least connected with the kidnapping of the girl."

I nodded. "It has to be something Chief. The first car follows Doc, the second car joins in. Something is up it can't be coincidence. Doc's son is the boy they were going to sacrifice? The girl a few nights ago? Jesus what the fuck are we into here?

"If it was a coincidence, we should all go buy Lotto. I go by the book Jimmy." He continued, "I believe in due process. When I lock someone up, I know it is likely going to change their lives and not for the better. I do the best I can to make sure it is warranted. I don't beat confessions out of people and I act a certain way and I expect my cops to act a certain way. But I also do not approve of people who rape kids and film it, and kidnap them to sacrifice them on altars. I don't want my guys here yet, in case..."

"To make sure these people don't see them and run," I finished for him, letting him know that I understood what came after in case and that I agreed with it.

"It's understood, Chief. And I can speak for Doc and Smitty we are on the same page and I have no problem helping you get that information, if need be. Especially if it turns out they are following Doc to find his son. And why 5 guys if they aren't going to try and take him? Contrary to popular belief violence isn't my preferred method, but I don't mind leaning on someone when kids are at stake." I trailed off.

He nodded and smiled.

"Don't say it. Todd was asking for it," I said.

"Boy did he get it."

"I wasn't exactly fit as a fiddle after."

"Well it's a bitch getting old."

"Have you considered comedy when you retire Chief? You are fucking hilarious." I tried to keep a stern face but I couldn't help laughing. He grinned at me. "Oh fuck, that son of a bitch is still with me, it takes me a half an hour to get up sometimes. I had to take a pain killer just to work out light the other day."

"Have an eye on that Jimmy," He said. He had spent too much time telling people that their loved ones had Od'd in the basement.

"I use it when I need it pal, that's it. Although I do need it more as I'm getting older."

"Like I said, it's a bitch," His radio popped. He spoke into it and put it next to his ear. "Plain clothes guys will be here in 2."

"There's an alley on the side, see it?" I asked him.

"I do."

"How about we get them out into the alley. There aren't cameras there."

"And how do we know this?"

"We were asked to install a security and camera system here. The owner of place goes to Smitty's school."

"I've stopped by to see Smitty a few times, he has some very funny stories about you and him working together. He's very proud of you."

I smiled. "If there are good things in me, he put them there."

"There are, Jimmy."

"Thanks, Chief." We had a good view into the pizzeria. "About the guy that is in there with the baby face," I began

"That's Joe. He turns out of the precinct. He's one of mine we've been texting. Good idea that about him pretending to be Doc's son."

"He was there with Smitty. I figured it would make Doc secure. He can handle himself just fine. He's got the nerves of a trauma surgeon but we don't want anything happening to his hands. Despite his nerves, he's worried and angry someone is targeting his kid, the boy is still dealing with the trauma he suffered," I said. "Joe looks like he's seventeen," I said.

"Twenty-three. We use that to our advantage. It fast tracks him and he is fine with that." I didn't ask if he could be trusted that was what "He's one of mine" meant. Doc sat with Joe, the guy pretending to be his son and I asked him "Any suggestions as to how we might get these guys to relocate into the alley?

The five mutts sat together. They had no idea apparently we were there or that I had followed him. I thought for a few seconds.

"Well aside from gun point, they have seen me. I can go in there. Sit with Doc and his son, look at them, let my face register I recognized them and hustle Doc and Joe out the side door that leads into the alley."

"And if they don't follow?" he asked.

"I don't know Chief, any suggestions?"

"Yeah. I'd say we roust them and take them in. But the problem is," he started.

"They haven't done anything and although they have acted suspiciously you could stop them but if they turnout clean and keep their mouths shut you'd have to let them go."

"Sounds like a plan, we need to do something," I said. "I'm ready when you are."

I stared at the 5 guys in the Pizzeria. They looked more like ex cops than they did thugs although being considered a thug myself by some, (I like to think a benevolent thug), sometimes there wasn't a big difference. I could see them well enough so that the guy I pegged as the leader was looking at his phone, he seemed to start and look around. I don't know how I knew, but I did.

"Chief put the plain clothes guys on their cars right now trust me," I said as I reached for my phone. I had a joint text with Smitty and Doc going. "If they leave tell the m to follow them and be careful they will be looking."

One thing about Mike, he knew me. I knew my job. I had done it a long time. Sometimes I went by my guy but most of the time I was right. "No one moves if they leave. Don't even look at them," I said using speech to text. Don't get me started on that. How it got sentences like "Okay see you then" as "Okay Love you hun" which, yes I sent to a client, but got words like hermaphrodite right (never mind why I used that word) I'll never know. But thank God it got that sentence right. As the five guys got up, both Smitty and Ken looked at their phones and didn't move when the fabulous five just got up and left.

"Copy," I heard Mariano say into the radio. "Watch out, these guys may be looking for a tail be careful, I need to know where they end up."

He looked at me briefly before he watched the five leave in their two cars. "We now have two cars on each and they will follow them. It's all we can do."

"What the hell's going on?" he said as the cars pulled away.

"I'll bet you anything they were warned. They had no idea we were here. The guy I think is the leader looked at his cell and then looked around just before they left."

We were quiet until Mariano spoke again, ten seconds later. "They were warned."

14

ALTHOUGH I KNEW we had thwarted a kidnapping, I didn't know how. Somehow I knew I had tipped them off to Sam. I had an interest in the occult when I was a kid but now that ended with watching The Exorcist. I needed an expert and although my client knew about it, I needed outside help. In my car I called Marc MacYoung. Marc is the Albert Einstein of violence, he had testified for me on some cases I handled, about self-defense. He had been qualified in numerous courts not just as an expert in self-defense but in violence and in several sub categories. We had talked one evening about strange things and he mentioned a friend of his I met once. He picked up on the first ring.

"Hey there Sunshine what can I do you for?"

"Macula. How goes it?"

"All's well. Tell me what you need I am about to consume mass quantities."

I laughed. "Is Clint Jahn around? Might he still be in New York State?"

"He and Queen are."

"We got trouble and I need him."

"Esplain."

I told him as condensed a version as I could. He listened until I finished.

"Jesus, Jimmy."

"Yeah. Before they get another kid I need to know what is going on," I said.

"I would say you do. They might be able to help. Your client is too close to this. Yes. There may be something he missed. I mean you know you have whackos that get off on hurting kids but it feels like it's layered, that there might be something else at play," he responded.

"Well to an extent I only need to know that they are hurting kids but as far as capabilities, goals, motivation and such, it might be good to know more."

"Knowledge can never hurt, that is for sure," he said.

"Agreed. Tell you what, get hold of him for me. Tell him I got him covered for a good rate of pay, I need him and Queen a few days. Tell him to get here, I'll arrange a good room for them at the Hilton. They are on the clock as soon as they leave for here. I guarantee them a minimum of 3k for two days. I want you to make the call to pay me back for that favor I did for you after you did that favor for me and so on."

He laughed. "Meaning he'll go if I ask him."

"I think he'd come anyway because of the kids but you know him longer and I need him."

"Done."

"I'll send you a gratuity and I promise not to tell people you are actually Bob Seger."

"Damn it that is supposed to stay between us!"

"It will." I laughed.

"If he comes," we both said at the same time.

"Black mailing SOB!"

"Thanks, pal, I love ya."

"You got it. Talk soon."

————

WE ALL ENDED up at Sophia's home a few hours later. A few more of Ham's security people joined him. I knew Terry Trahan and Clint Overland. Ham had apparently been reading a book with the title "The View From Flyover Country" by someone named Steve Browne. He was discussing it with a sky scraper that had apparently learned to speak and wear clothes. I stood next to Mariano. He was about six foot and well-muscled. I am a couple of inches shorter and I'm built heavy. I currently weighed two forty-eight. We looked like little kids next to most of the guys in the house. Jeff came with Ray Gordon who was six five and Sly who was six three. Doc came with his father and Sam. Sam went to find Ham's kids. Doc told me he had a few of his father's people watching his home where the rest of his family was. I knew Terry Trahan and Clint Overland from work, they were in from Texas for a few months like they had been ten years ago. Terry was average but Clint also ran about six five and maybe three hundred pounds with no waist. We had actually worked on opposite sides of a case some years back and things worked out well because both of us were there. I had the feeling I might be asked to sit at the kiddie table.

I don't know how Sophia managed to have all the food she did but everyone was eating including the detectives that were working the case from the angle of the kidnapped girl. It was almost like a party and under any other circumstance I'd have had a great time. They were my people; people I could relate to. The Grants had two beautiful older dogs that everyone lavished with attention. Mariano and I had foregone going home or stopping to eat but we did get two large coffees at Dunkin Donuts and two donuts each. We ate in his car and discussed things for a bit.

"Someone Ham knows is in on this," he said.

"Has to be," I agreed.

"Inside info, but he knows these people," he said.

"He does," I agreed again. "He has his house swept."

"Yep," he said.

"We should still be careful of sharing details in the house."

He looked at his cell phone. "Both cars and all five guys are at a hotel in Travis," he said after reading it. He texted back that he wanted the place watched and he wanted enough people there in wait to deal with them. "See if you can find out when they are leaving," he said into his phone and then apparently had to fix some of the words that speech to text got wrong. At least it wasn't only me.

Mariano, his detectives and his driver, myself, Vivian from Ham's crew and a guy named Tom Manfre (both retired cops), Jeff and Ray Gordon, Doc and Smitty, Ham and Sophia all went briefly into what turned out to be a laundry room, although it was cramped and a little noisy I had chosen it because the washer and dryer were on.

"I think we should get the three kids out of here, to be safe," Mariano said. "While we figure out where, we will keep all three under guard here."

"I fully concur," I said. "We should keep the people at Doc's house also. Maybe we get another lead, one of them, whoever them is, shows up there."

"If you think that is best, absolutely," Doc said. I knew Sophia and Ham were aboard because I had suggested it to them earlier.

"No one outside this room can know about any of this," I said. Smitty stepped away and made a couple of phone calls.

Ham and Sophia looked at each other. Ham shrugged. "The fewer people know about something like that the better," he told his wife.

"You don't think someone we know has something to do with this?" Sophia asked her husband and me at the same time.

"We have to treat that as possible. I know my people are clean. The Chief knew both Vivian and Tom from the job. But then again," I said, "there is some kind of fanatical, cult thing going on here."

"It's hard to think about," Tom Manfre said. "These guys, they are all good people. We all broke in on that ceremony that night. I tell you Chief," he said looking at Mariano. "That was one of the worst things I've ever seen. What they were doing to that little boy, keeping Elias and Steff in that cage." He shook his head. "When they told me ballistics came back, I'd killed this guy with his knife raised," he was quiet a moment. "I felt not one ounce of remorse."

Vivian was obviously thinking about it also. I had the first chance to really notice her. She had long red hair and her face more than met the definition of beauty. She was kind of hard to describe but there was also, aside from the pleasant visage, something that indicated depth, in her face. She was tough no doubt, but had seen and felt a lot of pain. That added to her beauty rather than subtracted from it. And when she smiled, which wasn't often enough, she lit the room. Bill Sebastian the lead NYPD Detective joined us.

"Well you all know the details now," I said. "Ham it has to be that someone in your life is involved in this. I don't buy that ten years ago it just so happened those cult members with that symbol showed up across the street from where you worked. Okay so, most reported Satanic Crimes are hoaxes. Very few are actual crimes and of those for the most part, they are freaks that enjoy hurting children. That incident? Just like when Ham was a child, you got true believers in that mix. Now even if that is the coincidence of all coincidences, that fucking girl, runs out in front of Ham's fucking car just as he, one of a half million of the Island's residents, is driving by?"

No one said anything.

"I came to the same conclusion," Sebastian said.

Sophia looked genuinely heart broken. I knew that she and Ham saw their crew as family. Someone, a member of their family, had betrayed them.

"My God," Sophia said, almost in tears. "Who could do that?"

"An utterly ruthless person," Mariano answered softly.

"And whoever it is, they have a reason, there is selection and design in this, planning that went on for years, at least I perceive it to be so," I said. "Whoever it is, they are getting a steady stream of information. I left here, stopped off for a haircut, grabbed a hot dog and went to Doc's office. Then at that exact time five people show up, almost certainly to grab Sam. Did they follow me to both places, both cars and I didn't pick up on them?"

"It sounds more like they got info on Doc and Sam," Sebastian said. "Did they learn it earlier or is there a bug the sweep missed or someone planted it after or did someone that was here let them know?"

A lot of questions, I thought. Not many answers. "Ham," I said. "The reason we are talking in here is because I want your house swept again. And I want your car checked. Sophia's and the one Elias has also. Your computers, everything. I have a message into my guy, as soon as he can be here, we need it done. It'll be an expense but we have to check."

"We did get new appliances last month," Sophia said. "We have had a little work done too. "My daughter's room was painted and we did have two occasions with a lot of people over and we had one of them catered."

"Okay," Ham said, dismissing the money aspect away with a wave. "But why not," he began.

"Sweetheart," Sophia said, putting her hand on his shoulder. "Let him do what he needs to."

He was likely going to ask why it couldn't be his normal guy.

Ham nodded. He looked dejected. Vivian and Tom moved off to speak with Sebastian. Mariano and I spoke with Jeff and Ray Gordon, remaining in the room.

"Hey Jimmy, who can we eliminate or probably eliminate from these people?"

"Clint and Terry. I know them. Everyone that was in this room. All of my people."

"How about, we work the room?" Mariano suggested. "Let's talk with everyone else.

Doc spoke up. "Ham, think for a second. Did anyone else know about Sam? Think hard. I wouldn't ever fault your judgement. But in all this time was there anyone else? That knew?"

Smitty paid special attention as his grandson's name was in play in the discussion. Ham did not have to take a moment to think he answered right away.

"Absolutely not," he said. Sophia nodded. "Kerik told us he didn't like the feel, how the leader got away. The similarities. We never even discussed it here. The kids knew but they are well beyond their years when it comes to this. They remember how vicious those animals were. The kids never even discussed it among themselves. Sam is still plagued by the fear someone is coming to get him."

"Never discussed it?" I asked.

"No," Sophia said. "We treated it like taboo. Not even in passing."

"Can we speak with you and the Chief, Jimmy?" Smitty asked me. Everyone else but Ham took that as a cue to leave.

"We will go work the room," Jeff said. "Whoever it is, is very smart, but we need to start somewhere."

"May I stay Sensei?" Ham asked.

"Of course, son. You're family, too. And you and your children are involved. It's a shame you and Jimmy never got to meet before this."

He took a breath and took a moment searching for the right words. "I am eighty. I could have a year left or I could have ten years left. I need to know my son and my grandchildren are safe. If you know who it is and you tell me, they will never make it to a jail cell. It doesn't matter to me."

No one said anything for a minute. You would hear lines like that in half the books you read, half the movies you see. The difference here? He meant it. No one doubted it.

"Dad," Ken said putting his hand on his father's arm. "We need you. Sam is going to have a hard time with this. We all need you."

"If it meant the safety of my grandson and Ham's two kids, I wouldn't mind going out that way. Once I got sentenced I'd just stop taking my heart meds."

"You have my word," I told Smitty. "If it looks like whoever it is, is going to skate, I won't just tell you, I'll help you."

Mariano said nothing, and Sebastian, he went up a few notches in my book because he said nothing either. Having gotten to know Mariano, if it was his kid, he'd do just as Smitty would.

"That will do then," he said.

"Well chief, we have three things to accomplish, the guys at the Hotel and the Sweep. And we have to figure out who in Ham's life is part of this. And if that person is here," I said.

"Don't forget we still don't know what "this" is," Mariano replied.

"Yeah."

"Who would gain something from the actions taken so far?" Doc asked.

We were all quiet for a minute. The washing machine did some kind of a rinse cycle and made a noise and we all looked at. I kept staring at it. Everyone kind of faded out as I stared at the machine. I did this sometimes. It was like everything was getting processed in the background. I went through Ham's book. It was like highlights of what I'd seen, read, heard and thought. Something was there. Let it out. Someone called my name. I raised my hand in an offhand way. I kept running through it.

Ham wasn't a suspect, it had to be someone close to him. It couldn't be Sophia. Well it could be but everything in me rejected that. Was it possible? No. But if it wasn't Ham it had to be someone super close. How did they have this info? Was it one of the kids? Who else was in his family? The house was swept. But they knew things. The car probably showed up after I left Ham's. We talked about Doc in the house. A bug? A camera? The Sweeper had missed? Family. Someone close to Ham was involved. They never found his brother. Who was with the freak that called the shots?

15

WE WORKED THE ROOM. I started interviewing people. I got that Ham currently had sixty regular guys that worked the clubs for him. Another forty part timers and fill-ins. Foster, Clarence, Dwayne and Carl all had the same figures. If the brother was involved, it couldn't be Clarence, Dwayne, Tyson of any of the other guys that were black or Hispanic. It couldn't be a woman. There were people like bartenders and managers at the clubs Ham knew well and saw socially. The brother, if I was right and taking into account age and he was almost certainly Caucasian to be one of twenty-five people. We had to narrow that list down.

Motivation. What would the motivation be? Clarence, Foster and Dwayne all got text messages about there being problems. Ham got them as well. The four of them talked and left. Ham had asked other people that worked for him that weren't working that night to come by.

I talked with them about the night in the city. They rarely talked about it among themselves, for the most part if a new employee found out about it was the only time.

"Ham is strong, you know? You put some gym time in," Carl had said to me.

"Yeah," I said.

"He pulled good enough weight he'd have made the US Olympic Team. He was only about forty pounds off the guys that were the best in the world in his division. I saw him deadlift over seven on a trap bar and I swear, it looked like it was cake for him. But even being that strong, it was unbelievable. I mean he picked that guy up and threw him maybe I don't know, ten feet? And the guy's body broke that stone altar they had. The rage he had for that much adrenaline," He shook his head. "He was in pain for two weeks after. Like he hyper extended everything doing that."

"Hell," Foster said. "Whenever there is a problem he ends up right there in the middle of it. He's not just strong he moves so damned fast. Some guy once fighting with his girlfriend. He picked up a bottle and we were at least twenty-five feet away and he moved and closed that distance so fast the rest of us had barely started."

"Hell we have one hell of a crew but Ham, he leads from the front," Dwayne said.

"Is there any of the other guys, any of his or some of the club employees that don't lie him?"

"Hell no. He watches out for everyone. One night we had a problem I got popped when some rich kid made a complaint. He was there with a lawyer and had me out on bond in no time. His lawyer got the case dismissed. If you want to see him move come one Sunday. Foster will probably do the knife thing again, too, we have a few new guys."

"Knife thing?"

"Ever see someone that really knows how to use a blade in action?"

"Oh yeah," I said.

"He's one of those guys. So is Terry. Clint is good with it and a few other guys but damned they move like,"

"Sewing machines?" I finished for him.

"Hell yes."

"Dwayne, who is he closest to? Ham I mean."

"Everyone. We got to barbeques, kids' birthday parties, and poker games. We are tight."

"Jimmy," someone said as they placed a hand on my back. Foster and Clarence stood there. Well Foster stood there. Clarence sort of became there. I smiled and raised my eyebrows. I saw Sebastian leave, likely headed for the hotel.

"Look we have a couple of problems at the club a few of us need to go there but we can head back when we are done and stay in touch," Foster said.

I remember pulling up the news articles. The picture in The Post of Ham and Foster. They had each killed someone. "Heroes" the caption read. Another had the whole crew in a photo that a newspaper got from online. The French Embassy people had celebrated their Independence Day at the club. They enjoyed themselves and felt so confident in the security they mentioned it on their website and had the picture of the crew.

Clint and Terry weren't just comfortable in violent

situations, they thrived in them. I was hoping to get more from them as well. Mariano came up to me.

"The guys at the Hotel. They were at the bar. One of my people listened in. They were making plans to leave about four A.M. and they went up to the suite that one of them rented. They are all on the fifth floor and the one we think is the leader of the group rented a larger room. My people are in position on the fifth floor and they have the stairs and the elevators covered. If they move, they will grab them. If not, they will wait until we get there."

"Mind if I come along?" I asked.

"That's why I'm telling you."

I left Jeff and Ray Gordon talking with the crew. I mentioned to Ham, Sophia, Doc and Smitty what we were doing. I whispered to Ham that my Sweep guy would be here tomorrow his guy might have missed something. No one but he and Sophia could know about it and they could tell no one. The only people that could be present were NYPD, my people and his immediate family excluding anyone from the business and they couldn't know about the sweep. I sent Dennis, the guy that handled the sweeps for me a message that I needed him here ASAP.

PART III

HAM ON CREED

16

WE MADE the ride over to the hotel in the Chief's private car. It was a Corvette, some kind of special edition. Eric Clapton's newer version of "After Midnight" came through the speakers in a smooth and easy way. We both listened instead of talking for a good while.

"I prefer the newer version," he said.

"You are a man of excellent taste, Wereowance," I replied. "I prefer this version also. I once wandered into Iridium in New York City in the later eighties to find the bar nearly empty and I saw him play a set with Les Paul."

"Damn!" the Chief said.

"Sadly, I was on a foot tail. I was actually working for Jeff doing a matrimonial and his client was married to a doctor who worked at Bellevue. I lost them. To this day Jeff doesn't know I lost them because of losing myself in the music."

He laughed. "How old were you?"

"Twenty-one. And I did catch him on a later date. He

was 72. His wife was forty-eight. He had two mistresses. One was fifty and the other was forty-seven."

"Holy shit, what vitamins was he taking?" he asked, laughing.

I laughed as well. "I never found out, although I actually did try."

"Damn again."

"He died at one hundred and two. With a hooker."

"You're pulling my leg."

"No, that's the truth."

"Damn!"

"I am more than content to watch you guys at work, Chief, but if you need me to do anything name it."

"I won't be shy in that area, Jimmy.

————

WE GOT THERE and the parking lot was somewhat crowded. He tinned the valet and parked the car were he could get to it in a hurry and let a plaque in the window.

A young female cop, a black woman who looked in great shape met us.

"Did they move in yet?"

"Just a few minutes ago Chief. It's," she trailed off a bit and her eyes were cast down. "Detective Sebastian is in there now. He'll fill you in."

Mike decided rather than question her as she seemed shaken, to move forward immediately. I stayed in tow. After getting off the elevator we could see the cops and EMTs congregating down the far end of the building. A cop asked me for ID and Mariano said "He's with me." My heart started beating knowing that after everything so far, we could find anything including a dead kid in there. I passed two cops I had met after some moron attacked my date, Harden and Glass. Harden smiled at me and Glass nodded. I shot at them with my forefinger.

"Jimmy, you're in this and I want you there. Hands in your pockets, conversation to a minimum. No matter what we see."

"Done, Chief."

We walked into the room, it was a large write, I had taken out suites that size when I have traveled for work, so I could meet with people and be comfortable. I stood there next to Mariano. He was quiet. Looking at the horror of what was before us, with almost no reaction, like a surgeon, cutting into someone. He was processing everything.

I had not long ago killed a man, with my bare hands. I had months ago, had the worst and most violent fight of my life, I took a man's face and ran it along the broken glass in a window frame. I had been shot at, I'd worked on cases like this where horrible things happened to children, but I got the case well after what happened had happened. I had done a few missing person cases involving kids and I found a couple including a girl when some hard and bad things happened to her, but I got her back. I knew that there was far worse than what I was seeing, but I was still overcome by the horror of it.

"My God," came out of my mouth before I could stop it. It was slightly less embarrassing because my voice was low and deep as my throat felt constricted. I drew those two words out slowly, as if I subconsciously hoped or even summoned the aforementioned

Supreme Being, who might remove what was before me.

All five of them were dead. Crime scene techs had already arrived. Sebastian stood near the Chief, waiting his turn to talk. The one I thought must have been leader was dead from what appeared to be a self-inflicted gunshot, a piece of the top of his head gone and a crimson stain on the ceiling but he had a smile on his face. The other four—one in a chair, two on a couch, and one in the bathroom—were dead with no visible wounds. There were drinks all over the place. Five. And a pitcher. Poison? He poisoned them and they knew or didn't know? Then he shot himself? Next to one hand was the gun and in the other clenched hand was a cell phone. A tech was removing it. Mariano initially spoke to Sebastian, and I gathered the cops had heard a single gunshot and moved in. And then I followed Sebastian's gesture to the wall. And there in black and red paint was the symbol Ham had mentioned.

I managed to keep quiet. I reminded myself this was an NYPD investigation and I was here as a courtesy. I got a message from Dennis that he'd be there late after-noon tomorrow. His flight was due in from Florida in a few minutes; he just got service. I texted him back to let me know when he was on the way and I asked him to update me when he could, also to remove anything he found but to keep it to himself, if I wasn't there. As an afterthought, I asked him to please text me when he landed.

"Affirmative," he responded. Dennis was one of those guys that you really wish you could see more often, but both your schedules threw a monkey wrench into that. He was the best at what he did. He looked a little like L.Q. Jones or Chris Squire. Long flowing white hair and a white mustache but a youthful glint in his eyes. Texting my friend gave my mind a brief respite from what I was encountering.

"I want to see what is in that phone ASAP, yesterday," Mariano said to Sebastian who went to speak to the tech.

"Chief?"

"Yeah?"

"What the fuck is going on?"

"I don't know. But we better damned well figure it out, Jimmy. These people kill, commit suicide, and hurt children and they are doing something in my borough."

"And probably targeting my client."

"We need to figure this out."

"Yeah," I said. "We are looking at four dead by poisoning—murder or suicide—and one almost certainly dead by suicide. Am I reading it right?"

"Looks that way to me."

Sebastian looked at the phone for a few seconds, his intelligent face grave and impassive, like the Chief's. He came over and handed Mariano a pair of gloves. He put them on and gingerly handled the phone in a way the belied his rough and scarred hands, which were made for combat.

"Everything is gone, deleted. Except for two last incoming text messages." The earlier one might have been the reason for the smile on the dead man's face. The smile he bore as he blew his goddamned brains out.

Thank you my faithful acolyte for all you've done. You will sit at the right hand of our Father and I will see you again.

My pride in all you have done, what you have become and
accomplished, and my pride in your faith and loyalty
cannot be measured in mere human terms. You have my
deep love, loyalty, and respect. You will never be replaced
and wills stand as a shining example for the faithful.

The words came out of me again. No stopping them.
"My God."

The second text resulted in us leaving. Mariano
called one of the cops back at Ham's as I called Jeff.

Good evening. I am unsure as to who exactly will receive
this. I would imagine it would be Deputy Chief Mariano
and Mister Creed, among others. If they by chance are not
here please get this to them ASAP, you are (please pardon
the bon mot) after all, public servants. I shall be contacting
Hamilton tomorrow, about four in the afternoon. I apolo-
gize for not providing a more exact time, but my schedule
is, as I imagine you would understand, in flux. It doesn't
matter where he is, and it doesn't matter who he is with, so
please do not let me inhibit your schedules, you can go
about your business. Good Night. Love, the Father

The ride back to Ham's was about fifteen minutes. I
faded out for the entire time and ran the new information gained through the texts through and revisited
what I knew. I heard Mariano somewhere in the
distance call my name.

"Just give me a minute, Chief," I murmured back.

Dennis texted me he had landed. I looked up and
realized we were back at Ham's parked outside. I texted
back, asking if he could call me. He responded he would
call from the car.

I knew what was going on and who it was. When I say knew, it would be more accurate to say I had formed and opinion based on everything.

Mariano and I looked at each other and I knew that he knew also. He nodded seeing that I had a theory. He spoke first.

"I think I know," he said.

I nodded. "Me, too. You go first."

"I thought from earlier today it had to be, but the messages confirm it for me."

"The messages put the thought in my head," I said. "You beat me to it."

"If what we *know* is the truth, and if we *know* the same thing," he said. "It's Ham's brother."

I nodded. "It has to be. Now the question is, who is Ham's brother?"

"We can figure that out through process of elimination."

"I think I know, but Dennis will confirm it for me. If he doesn't I'm probably wrong. But, if he confirms it and I get the answer I am expecting from a few more questions, I know who it is. Let's not jump ahead, I need more. I don't want to be hampered with tunnel vision."

"I have an idea but I'm not a hundred percent certain as you appear to be."

"Let's hold off on that then," I suggested. "I don't want tunnel vision yet."

He nodded.

Dennis called. "Jimmy. How are you?"

"I'm good. Dennis I know you must be exhausted but this thing has taken some turns, people died and more could die. How soon could you get here and do your thing?"

"I have my equipment Jimmy and my assistant is in the car next to me but we haven't slept in a long while."

"Where are you?"

"About an hour from home, just getting to the Goethals Bridge." He lived in Nassau County.

"Could you get a room on the Island? I'll pay for it. Then when you are ready you are ten minutes away."

He sighed the sigh of a man that had worked hard and needed to get home to his wife. I hated asking him this because he had just finished up another round of preventative chemo and although he kicked cancer's ass, he had just started working again.

"You really think more people might die?" he asked.

"Yeah," I said. "Maybe children."

I heard him speak softly to whoever was in the car with him. "We'll grab a room at the Hilton Garden Hotel on South Avenue." He responded when he got the response from his assistant.

"I know the Nicotras fairly well, and the staff there," Mariano said. I'll call ahead.

"Did you hear that?" I asked Dennis. I knew the Nicotras also but I wasn't the NYPD Chief in charge of a borough.

He responded he did, expressed his appreciation and then he hung up.

"Even if it gets him here an hour earlier, it'll help," I said.

Mariano nodded. "How good is he?"

"The best," I said. "Okay. If there is any more of a delay, I can get someone from the department to do it but we have other things we can do in the meantime."

Mariano made the call to the hotel and he told me

after they were waiting for Dennis, to mention his name. I texted Dennis that information.

My phone rang. It was Clint Jahn. "Hey!"

"Jimmy how are you?"

"I'm good pal. I'm glad you're here. How are you guys?"

"We just got here after an 8-hour ride. Tired but okay. Marc filled me in."

"You're at the Hilton?"

"Yeah?"

"Perfect. My sweep guy is going to be checking in, get some rest and you guys can come with him or follow him over tomorrow. I'll have a check ready for you."

"Thank you, we'd have—" he started.

"Come for free because of the kids. I know. But my client is a good man and he has the money and he will pay. If I need help I'll tell you. I'm getting paid here and so will you."

"Great."

I bade him sleep well, and we hung up.

ALTHOUGH IT WAS LATE, the people at Ham's for the most part, worked night time. As soon as I walked in to my great surprise and actual happiness, I saw some old friends. Tony Dasaro. He along with Smitty had been one of my teachers when I was young. He was a Doctor now, an internist. He had been back in New York, went to see Smitty and learned of what was going on and came here. We talked for a bit and I made him promise that we'd find a few hours before he left and catch up.

Jeff Greico who was a good friend and a longtime training partner had retired from PD as a lieutenant, and last I heard was taking tango lessons. I tried to get him to work with us but he planned to actually retire. None of us would remain retired if Smitty needed us.

Smitty grabbed me and asked me to go outside.

"I got a property, with a house I just bought upstate. I have a half dozen good, hard people that are armed or I can arm that will come. We can take the kids and they'll be safe there."

"Great idea," I said. "How far?"

"Couple of hours," he said. We can be there before the sun is up and we can leave now, I won't say where in the house."

"Is everyone here?" I asked.

He shook his head. "Those people that left, the giant and the other guys they went to some of the night clubs. But they have been in touch."

I nodded and followed him into the house. He grabbed everyone he had in mind, including Tony and Jeff as well as Ham and Doc and brought them outside, away from the house. Mariano was moving around asking questions as were other members of PD. I grabbed Sophia and we went into the laundry room again.

"I know how you met Ham, from his book but had you ever talked to him or anyone else from the club before that night where you officially talked. Even a bartender."

From years of asking questions and seeing reactions I saw she was troubled. She wanted to say something but wasn't sure. I saw from her eyes she was troubled.

"Sophia, anything at all, it could be important."

"Well Manny the bartender I knew from going there. And, well I never told Ham, but..." She paused. "Look, I don't want him to know this unless he has to, okay?"

"Only if he has to," I assured her.

"Foster had told me that Ham was into me. That he had a hard life and was a great guy and he kept talking about me. He said Ham was like his brother and he knew he might be really nervous because he really liked me. When we were talking. Manny agreed. He was tending bar and he brought me a drink. On the house.

He said Ham really was a great guy. I was at the point in my life where I had promises broken and was tired of people, but I still wanted to meet someone. And I did give Ham the chance and I'm so happy I did. He is such a good man, and I have no idea why he turned out so good. He loves our kids. Come to think of it, a few times after Manny had inquired if anything had happened and when it did they were both very happy for us."

Although I had faded out a little again, I smiled. Distantly still connected to her, I spoke softly and put my hand on her arm. "It's because although he was brutalized, he was still brought up by people that loved him, taught him to be good."

"I understand if you need to tell him" Sophia said. "But Jimmy, he doesn't think he deserves us, to be happy. He has so much hurt in him. He still cries over his brother sometimes. He's paid people to see if they could find him or find out what happened to him."

"If I do need to tell him, it will be necessary and you'll understand," I told her.

She smiled, nodded and kissed me on the cheek. Then she went off to find her husband. I joined Mariano in working the room.

Terry Trahan was telling me about the Sunday morning training sessions. "I'll tell you this, Foster? He told me he was in the military over-seas. I make him out to be SAS or SBS. He uses a knife like it was part of him. We did this thing for the new guys. One of them wore an old flannel shirt, Foster had a permanent magic marker and we told the new guy to take the knife. In seconds that old shirt was covered with marker.

I went back to my office and slept for a few hours. I had texted my friend Cheryl to please take care of Molly in the morning. She was up and I promised her another donation to the Staten Island Council For Animal Welfare as she refused to take money from me.

Mariano had gone home and most of Ham's people had slept there. The Grants had a big home with a lot of spare rooms, a finished basement, and attic and multiple bathrooms. Apparently a lot of people had slept there. His extended family of choice was top notch.

Except for one of them, I thought. I had taken a quick shower at the office and I kept an emergency change of clothes. I didn't have a razor, though, and I still looked tired. Mariano showed up with a driver and looking like he had slept well and long, though he couldn't have.

Smitty had taken his people and some of Ham's and they all left. Only Mariano, myself, Ham, and Doc had the location. Mariano had called the local cops and asked for help. The kids would have a great time upstate. And they had some crew looking out for them. Another man, an older guy who looked to be about Jeff's age and had the bearing of a cop or a military man showed up. Ham hugged him. It was Walter Hertman, the cop that rescued him. His grip was like a vice but restrained. Ham had run to him and hugged him.

Mariano asked to speak with him. Cop to cop was always the way to go if you could. He'd fill me in.

Dennis showed up and went right to work, Clint and Queen followed him to the house. They were one of the coolest couples that there is and they looked it. Clint was shorter than average and wiry. He had the coiled energy of the last lug nut on a car that was about to pop. His head was neatly shaved and he had an honest to

God hook where his right hand should have been. Queen was taller than he, tall for a woman, and she moved with grace like a dancer and had a regal bearing that suited her name. She'd had a mohawk when last I saw her, but it was growing out. We were automatically allies through our belief in Vachss and our hatred of predators. Clint did security work, Queen did various vocations, and they were both authors. I had spent an evening with them in Colorado a few years ago and by the time it was over I had two more family members.

I had told Mariano that the Jahns had expertise in the occult and he had copies of the files with him. I found Clint and Queen a room and gave them everything we had including Ham's manuscript. I had highlighted the parts of the manuscript dealing with the Ham's experience with the subject. I also quietly told him I suspected that there were bugs and maybe video and not to say anything he wouldn't want the other side to know about. Dennis and his assistant made several trips and carried bags and metal cases in. He asked for Ham's phone, all the computers, and keys to the cars. He went off to do his work.

Not more than an hour later he called sent me a text telling me he was in the master bedroom to come up for a minute.

"We got two, don't worry the rest of the room is good." He pointed to a painting. "Video in the painting and audio in the light switch. Tied into the house's Wi-Fi in a separate VPN."

"Why wouldn't the sweep guy find it? Any reason?"

He shook his head. "A novice would have found it. Odds are your guy doing the sweeps is planting them.

And they can access them real time or catch up anytime they want."

"Jesus, Mary and Joseph," I said. "Let me know when you are done."

He nodded.

I went downstairs and got Mariano. I told him. He nodded. He told me that Walt had tried really hard to find the brother. No luck. He kept looking even after he retired. I motioned Ham over to us.

"Ham, who does your sweeps? I meant to ask you but didn't in the confusion."

"Manny, the bartender from the club. It's his day job. He does the club, my office, and here. Half the time he refuses to take money. He and Foster have been friends for years. He kind of looks at Foster like an older brother or something."

In time everyone from the prior night had returned except Foster, he'd left word he had to stop at the cub but would eventually make it back and we could call his cell if we really needed him. He had called Ham to make sure Ham didn't need him immediately and Ham reassured his friend it was all good. We all sat in the living room and I had them describe the scene, those that were there, when they broke in on the freaks mutilating Sam. Foster shot the guy that called out Father, was something they all recalled, with the pride that you'd expect. Ham seemed like a superhuman presence, hurling the freak presiding over the ceremony like he weighed nothing. I could hear Sophia cry several times when they spoke of the kids.

I KNEW THESE THREE GIRLS. They were nicknamed The Three Princesses. I also knew a guy named John Luchic and a PI in Boston named Don Pickard. They were all deep info specialists. I told them all I needed backgrounds on Foster and Manny. I got as much info as I could give them. Mariano did the same thing. They called back, switched up something and were coming. My office was only ten minutes away and the conference room was more than big enough. We relocated there. Everyone knew, not a sound when the call was on.

We were in my conference room. Ham sat at the head of the table his cell phone resting on the table next to a cup of coffee I had given him. There were a few uniformed cops in the room and two of Mariano's detectives just arrived. One of them was the sergeant in charge of the squad. We shook hands. A young female cop came in and went to Mariano and said something to him in a low voice. He responded and nodded his head toward the carafe with the coffee in it. I had also put pastries that had been brought to the office earlier in the day. Someone had gone to Renato's.

"Well shit if I can't figure out for sure who is trying to destroy my client's life and family, at least I can be a good host." That thought made the coffee I sipped bitter. It was two minutes to four. The "Father" was someone who all indications were, he'd call at four. On time. His time.

Most people I dealt with weren't smart. There were professional and amateur criminals, but still, unless you were talking like Bobby Bianchi—and I didn't person- ally consider him to be a criminal—no one was going to split the atom. Stanton had been clever enough that he was able to murder Mandy, but he was more clever than intelligent. And he was a freak; 99 plus percent of the bad guys would have run in his place.

At four, a phone was going off on the building phone system. It was my third line. Robo call. The service wouldn't pick that line up. We stared at Ham's phone. The young female cop that came in looked at my line that kept ringing. She was pretty but she already had that hard look real cops got, from dealing with the worst humanity had to offer. If she was working on something Mariano was in charge of, she'd be good.

"Chief," she asked softly. "How good is this guy? Does he have the capability to find out that phone number?"

Mariano and I looked at each other. The damned line was still ringing. I took the phone on the confer- ence room table and slid it toward Ham. I adjusted the volume on it and I told him to just push the blinking button and it would come on. I suddenly got a chill and was not expecting it to be a call about social security disability.

"This is Ham."

An electronic voice answered. "This is Father on a recorded line." The voice chuckled slightly.

"I'm here as you asked," Ham said.

"Of course you are. And good evening to your friends and would be protectors. I have a few minutes, I blocked some time out. This call can't be traced and I don't mind if they join in."

We were all silent. I looked at Mariano and he was thinking the same thing I was. We both knew but at the same time, what the hell were we dealing with?

"Let's start with something basic," I said. "What do you want?"

"Is that Creed?" Another chuckle. "Really, Jonathan. I thought that was obvious. I want Ham."

"Why? What do you want with him?" I asked.

"Very mundane but I guess it had to be asked, although I'd have thought that was obvious also. There are several reasons. But I will answer, and although I will reserve judgement, you are heading towards being classified as a disappointment, Jonathan."

When I was younger and it was obvious I had an aptitude for this work, I used to lament that I never found my Moriarty. I'd tell people if there was something there and I had the resources (if my client had the money) and the time to do it I'd find a way. Tense moments but no huge problems. Now at this stage I'd have been content not to find him.

He sighed. "Sustenance."

"Jesus Christ," one of the cops said.

"Oh, no sir. Wrong direction."

"Explain that, please."

"Ahh, Deputy Chief Michael Mariano. You are polite even to the likes of me.

"Everyone is entitled to courtesy."

"Yes, until they demonstrate otherwise. In my universe, Chief Mariano, God and Satan are reversed. Satan presents the true nature of humanity."

"What do you mean sustenance?" Mariano asked.

"I feed off the pain of others. Pain is good, it shapes us, it's a driving force. In Ham's case, however, as I gave him the life he does not deserve, he has a debt now."

I saw Clint and Queen listening intently. Each of them had a notebook and was scribbling intermittently. Clint seemed intent on the phone call but it appeared to me that Queen's attention was fixed on Ham.

"Why Ham?" I asked. "Because he broke in on your followers?"

"Creed. What a disappointment. Really, Ham, this is the best you could do? Him? It should have been a sign to you. If he couldn't protect his own woman, why would he be able to protect yours? You would have been better off just dealing with me yourself."

Mariano watched me. He was and should have been concerned that would affect me. It did, but I brushed it off. Outwardly. Let me get my hands on you mother fucker, was what I thought. Clint motioned to me. We stepped just outside the door and he spoke softly to me.

"Something is wrong here. Half, no more than that, three quarters of this stuff is bullshit. I don't have time to explain it, but there is no Satan. This is like someone watched a bad 70s movie and built up a cult around what Hollywood thinks Satanism is. But some things that are real, that a genuine practitioner would know and do. That symbol or that mish mash of symbols, it's nonsense. The sustenance thing, that's no joke. I believe he's invited something in and that's how it feeds." We stopped because Mariano was talking now.

"Then I will ask," Mariano said. "Why Ham."

Slight pause. "You are asking me these questions because you believe you will learn who I am and then you'd be able to find me. How disappointing. You won't find me that way. I don't exist in your world. But Ham belongs to our master, our father, he was born into his service."

"See," Clint said to me. "That's bullshit. It's a cover. Its misdirection. He is a true believer."

"In what?" I asked. Queen still stared at Ham.

"I'm not entirely sure. But I'm certain something shares his body. He is intentionally misleading."

"Wait," I whispered. "That makes sense he has these followers, baby rapers, freaks they have some kind of Hollywood inspired idea about Black Masses and he believes in something different. They're pawns, he uses them. Maybe a few like the guy that blew his brains out after poisoning the other four are inner circle."

Ham stared at the phone. One of the cops made constant notes in his book. I knew and Mariano knew but we wanted more information.

"Yeah okay, Clint but people are dying here. They are killing people and committing suicide."

Queen had moved closer and spoke in agreement. "That's what I think it is," He is a true believer. He probably has a few true believers around him, the rest he feeds this Hollywood bullshit to, and they're freaks that like raping kids to begin with. He likely uses that, the kiddie porn for revenue."

"You keep looking at Ham, Queen. Something occur to you?"

"I have a very strong feeling they are going to clash. Ham is driven, and I can sense it's going to happen."

"What? Like they are going to confront each other? One lives the other..."

"Yeah," she whispered.

"Who are you?" Ham asked. "Why me?"

"We are connected Ham. You strayed from the path. Worse still, you failed in your role as a father. You have lead the children astray."

"I will do whatever you want. You can have me. Just leave my family alone." I was alarmed now. I could hear it in Ham's voice. He would do anything to protect his family. If this monster told him to drive his car off a cliff and he'd leave the family alone, Ham would do it.

"No Ham. Partial payment for what you have done is that I feed on your pain. I don't mean that I feel good by making you hurt Ham. I feed off your pain. Like I said. Sustenance." Another pause. He did that to let the t of what he said sink in. "It is the least of what you owe me."

"Because he shut down your pathetic little church?" I asked moving closer.

Another laugh. A cold electronic laugh. "No. Among his transgressions the greatest, is his lack of gratitude, I gave him this life. I even let him have my children."

There was a full minute of silence. My jaw had dropped. Mariano and I looked at each other and then we both looked at Ham. The kids he found in the cage. They were this freak's children. I didn't need a DNA test to know this was true. I knew. And knew who it was. Clint edged in and spoke into my ear.

"It might help if we can ask him questions."

"I don't want this freak knowing about you guys. I know you can take care of yourselves but he has a lot of money behind him and followers. He's got this whole Jim Jones thing going on. I don't want that on you."

I turned my attention back to Foster. "You gave up any parental right you had, you son of a bitch, by putting your children in a cage. You're no religious icon, mother fucker," I said. "You are a freak that likes hurting children. And you use all this as window dressing," I said.

"Wrong, simpleton," the voice said to me. "I do feed off pain. The pain of innocents is especially potent but I believe. I am not just a follower I am his representative, his vessel."

"I will tell you what, Father," I said. My hands on the table facing the phone and wishing I had my hands around his throat. But I had succeeded and I did make him mad. He wasn't going to tell us anything he hadn't decided to. He would have spent hours going over the pro and cons of what he would reveal. He hadn't achieved his objective and he'd be careful not to sabotage himself and his objectives. But I sensed something, through the electronic voice disguise and his carefully measured responses. Arrogance. He'd not like being insulted by a lesser man. Maybe this way he would reveal something. I signaled to them I was trying something. Mariano nodded.

"I have a special clip that I keep with me. It's loaded with Glasers. When I find you, and I will, I am going to empty that clip into you and you will become porous, you baby raping low life piece of shit, and as your life drains I'm going to force your mouth open, piss in it, and watch you turn into a fucking sprinkler."

A pause. At first I thought I read it wrong. Maybe he hung up. But then the laugh came. I could feel his anger but he damned sure wasn't going to show me.

"Amateur. It's a magazine." Bingo. Whatever he was, he was a pro. That's what the background checks said. He had been in the military. Terry said he was absolutely deadly with a blade. He killed his follower in New York ten years ago. The man wasn't calling out to Satan, he was calling to his leader. I had just read online some snob talking about guns and ammo. "Actually they are all magazines, clips are slang. As most of you haven't served, you wouldn't know that but now you do.

"Well, Ham," he continued. "We will get together soon enough. It should have occurred to you that you were bred to be of service. You can't have happiness. The only way you could is to give yourself in service to the true father and now it's probably hopeless. You have ruined years of work by corrupting the children. I have given you enough to make you afraid. I will go now. I have things to attend to. But remember this Ham," He said. Another laugh. "You failed as the children's father because you are not their father. I am. They are my property. You could have done better though. I would honestly have expected the children's uncle to raise them better in my stead."

I exhaled slowly. I looked at Mariano. He nodded. We had told Ham about the call and he was up to it.

"Why not turn off the electric voice and tell us who you are," I said.

"The game amuses me."

"I already know who you are," I said.

"Oh?"

"Yes you are Ham's brother. And for a long time you have pretended to be Ham's friend. You kept yourself in the background until you felt it was the right time." As I talked Dennis walked in. I made the motion to write it down.

"Well Creed, very good."

"But I also know more than what you are, I know who you are."

"Liar. You really think you can trick me into giving myself away before I want you to know?"

"I know who you are, Foster."

Everyone froze. The phone was silent. Ham stood there dumbfounded. It had to be. I knew it a long time ago. He shot his follower. He manipulated Sophia seeing the boy dragged from the car, the girl running in front of Ham's. It had to be.

"It's Foster?" Ham asked.

"Yes, Ham. I am your brother. I gave you everything you have. I sought to make you understand your role, what you were born for. I did apparently underestimate this man you hired and the Chief."

"We knew for a while, Foster," I said. "From their description what everyone missed was you killing your own follower ten years ago."

Dennis came over and handed me the paper and faded into the background. I read from it. "You put tracking devices on Ham's cars. You had listening devices and cameras in his home. Manny put them in. It was perfect. You knew, finally, who the other little boy was. You acted on that too quickly. All the signs were there. It just needed people that weren't too close to the situation to see."

"Well, I must say, give credit where it is due. Well done, Jonathan."

"I know something else, Foster."

"Do tell."

"You yourself are a true believer, of what I don't know. But you concocted this Satanism idea or the creatures that spawned you and Ham were being fed that. You dangle it like a carrot and get followers. Kiddie porn and who knows what else funds things. You believe in something dark and evil. In your mind you're aligned with it. The guy that blew his brains out for you, he believed, too, and he believed you were something special to whatever it is."

"Well, I am taken aback, Jonathan. That really is very good. You're close. You can call him Satan, there's not enough time to explain it and make you understand. For all intents and purposes, what you imagine Satan to be is what I serve. What Ham was born to serve."

I looked at the Jahns. Clint nodded.

"I don't suppose you want to come in and surrender," Mariano said.

"No, Chief. I have things to do. I was born with a purpose. My respect for your ability does not include my turning from the course."

"Foster, I want you to know, if you hurt another child I will kill you myself," I said.

"Unlike some of my followers, I get no pleasure hurting children. They are a sacrifice. But if that is what keeps my family happy, they are just children, born to serve his followers. The pain of the flesh is temporary." He gave a short harsh laugh. "Your system and your society, Creed, does not protect children. Why shouldn't

I use them? The political party in control calls those that hold intercourse with them MAPs. If you all really cared, it would never happen. Do you stop those that hurt them? Maybe. If you are paid."

"Enough of us care, Foster. And I promise you, if you hurt another child you will end up dead with your boss, Satan, Mammon, whatever the fuck it is, down in the fucking basement or in prison. Mark that down, fucker."

Ham had tears running down his face. Sophia had moved in and was hugging him.

"Billy," Ham said, moving closer to the phone. "We are brothers. Stop this. Let it end. Don't hurt anyone else."

"Ham. You are my brother. I do love you, but you are blind. You have a purpose. Come back to it. Make the right choice."

"You can't even call me by name, like I did you, Billy. They never even gave me a name. I was a possession."

"We all are, Ham. He will forgive you. I will forgive you. We can all be a family. We can leave, and they will never find us. I have backup plans, there's no chance I'll be caught. When you feel the power that comes from understanding, what it can do for you, you won't regret it. We can be a family. That's what you want."

Sly came in. He had listened apparently enough to catch up. Ray Gordon was with him. I looked at them and raised my eyebrows. They nodded. I breathed a sigh of relief.

"Foster, despite everything, you used to take care of Ham. You brought him food, blankets. You tried to help him. Be that brother again. Stop this. Please do not hurt any more children," Mariano said.

"You have been very courteous, Chief Mariano. I won't lie to you. Our Master demands his sacrifices. There have been many. We don't leave the shells where you can find them. And he rewards us for the tribute. I'm sorry. I do the best I can for them to feel no pain."

"You call carving a symbol into the chest of a child painless? Raping kids on video so you can sell it to other freaks harmless?"

"I drug the children when I can. The one we have now will sleep through it. If Ham declines, I will leave that child where she will be found and an autopsy will prove I have told you the truth."

"Billy," Ham began.

"My name is Foster, Ham."

"Foster. Please. Don't do this."

"You don't have much time, Ham. You'll have to choose. Life for you and your family in service to the true master, or I take from you what I have given. You cannot run or hide from me. Now you will all forgive me but have things to attend to. Decide, Ham. Soon."

The line went dead. Ham just stood there, frozen. My heart broke for him. His woman pulled him in and he went loose and allowed it. We left the room and gave them some time.

"Good to go?"

"Yup," Sly said with an ear to ear grin. "Second garage we checked."

"I have a feeling this will make me happy," Mariano said.

"Well, Chief, Ray and Sly went to the city, found Hamilton's Bentley and put a fully charged GPS on it."

"Damn, boys, I may even forget that is illegal," Mariano said with an ear to ear grin.

"Why I didn't mention it, Chief," I said.

"I hope you don't expect bail to be paid from the company coffers, Jonathan," Jeff said.

"Don't worry, pal, it's a billable expense."

Mariano took me by the shoulders and kissed me on each cheek. "Very good, Jimmy. I would work with you anytime."

"Thank you, Chief. If we get the chance, and it's at all possible, I would love to be the guy that—and again, only if the opportunity presents itself—drives Foster's teeth out the back of his head."

"That's a visual," Ray said, laughing.

"Something I picked up from Smitty," I said.

"If we don't get him," Sly said, "he will come after our man."

"No doubt about that," I said.

"I agree," the Chief affirmed.

"He's up to something," Queen said. "I think he was open about it. He's going to do something and disappear."

"He has the money to do that. Hundreds of millions if not billions inherited, and that fortune was built even more by him. He probably has a half a dozen identities with full back up and safe houses and money stashed all over."

"Plans, back up plans, and backups for the back-ups," Ray said, nodding.

"You're sure of this, Creed?" Sebastian asked me.

I nodded. "I had three separate deep backgrounds done on him. They all found that in the short amount of time we had. He probably has millions liquid."

"He has precious metals and gemstones available,

too. He could keep ten million in a single duffle bag," Ham said.

"Ham," Clint Jahn said softly. "We need to see you for a minute. Just a minute. It's urgent." Ham looked at me and I nodded. The three of them moved off to the corner. I saw Queen take his arm and close her eyes.

Sebastian's radio buzzed and he stepped away to be able to hear it. I went to the secretarial area and they followed me. Vivian and Tom Manfre made their way over also. We kept a laptop that I had connected to a large television-like monitor to see GPS devices. I got on it, pulled up the sight, and punched in the passwords and ID. It brought up a street grid superimposed with a satellite photo. The Jahns spoke and I saw Ham nod. Clint withdrew what looked like a stone on a chain, maybe an amulet, and Ham put it deep into his pocket.

Sebastian came back with bad news. "We had a child abducted an hour earlier. They left the mother for dead but she looks like she will pull through." The Jahns had moved closer, and Clint had a grim look on his face when Sebastian spoke of the abducted child.

As we looked at the screen, the Bentley stopped. It wasn't far from the college on Victory Boulevard.

"Jimmy," Jeff said. "Remember when Geraldo Rivera did the expose on Willowbrook?"

I nodded.

"There are still a huge number of abandoned buildings on the property."

"Yeah," I said.

"Not far from where Ham found the girl," Sebastian said.

"Okay, folks. He's probably got a kid. Let's head there. We'll stop on Victory Boulevard, here." He pointed at the map. "I'll call for ESU and more cops, but we are literally about two minutes from there."

When I asked Mariano if him allowing everyone to go on this field trip to a nightmare was going to cause a problem, he shook his head.

"If nothing goes wrong, who cares? These people are in this, we are in this. They all rescued those children in Manhattan. We are two minutes away. I want that kid, and my guy says I want them there. I wish Ham was carrying his fucking gun."

Queen was moving along. She caught up to Ham and held his arm for a few minutes and murmured a few words. There would be things that happened that night, that we all saw. Not all of us saw the same thing. I had no more problem with Queen doing whatever she did than I would if a priest had blessed one of us. As a matter of fact, I'd not have minded that at all.

Maybe a dozen cars brought us all over there. The Bentley with the tail pipe still hot was parked on a side street right where the GPS said it'd be and there was a small path in the woods visible.

"Fuck you, Foster," I said softly to myself. "Two can play at that game." Sly walked over and reached under the back of the car and took my GPS off.

"We have to get in there fast," Mariano said. "He is going to kill the kid and light out of here. If he gets out, we'll never find him again."

"Until he shows up, at a time he chooses to," Ham said. "I can't have that. He'll come for them." Sophia and a few of the other people stood about forty feet away. Ham had told her she had to stay there.

"Sophia, if you were there, he'd be concentrating on you and not what was going on or what he might have to do. You want him to be concentrating now, more than anything else."

"Okay," she said sadly.

Ray moved forward. "Chief, you, me, your people, and Jimmy, we'll go ahead by about fifty feet. Everyone else follows. Jeff, you lead the larger group. If I hold my hand up that means stop. When I want you to resume I'll motion forward. That's not the best way, Chief, but it's the quickest way."

"I want the child back alive," Mariano said to all. We moved out.

The moon gave us enough light so that we could see. Ray told everyone flashlights should be used only if needed because they could give us away if they had lookouts. God was on our side. We followed the path and it lead us to a cluster of abandoned buildings on the college property. From one of them faint light escaped from a window.

Mariano and Gordon conferred. They separated the group into smaller groups and directed some people to be outside, while some would be going in. The light that filtered from the building appeared to be coming from something like a Coleman lantern, but I could also hear the faint noise of a generator. An expensive one, but it would still make some noise. Ham insisted on being with us. Clint and Queen had a slight disagreement. I gathered that although Queen could take care of herself, she was staying behind. I agreed with Clint and got a look that made me a little afraid for doing so.

"Am I in trouble?" I asked him.

"Hell yes," Clint said. "But not as much as me."

"Good. While she is shredding you, I can run," I said.

"Queen is certain Ham and Foster are going to clash. She is never wrong about these things. Ham and Foster will settle this themselves."

"Please don't take offense, brother," I told him. "If I get the chance I'm going to send him off myself."

"No offense taken, and not if I get to him first," he said. "But she's never wrong."

Jeff addressed everyone. "Outside people, if you're not called in as re-enforcements, know this. There are tunnels around here, probably a dozen ways out. You can't let them past you."

Gordon and Mariano took the lead. The door to the building was closed, but we could hear voices. As we got closer, there was no question it was chanting. As we took up positions on either side of the door, Mariano and Gordon decided that Gordon, who had breached walls to compounds as a SEAL, would go in first. We were making ready and the goddamned door opened. A man in a robe came walking casually out. Gordon moved so fast I barely saw it. He yanked the man toward him and struck him. The guy fell in such a way that there was a good chance he wouldn't be getting up. We went in. The first room had coats hung up like it was a goddamned social club. Ham ran over to one of the coats, pulled a gun out, and gave it to Mariano.

"It's Foster's," he said.

"He have a backup?" I whispered.

"Not in this city, not legally," Mariano said.

"Is he obeying any laws at this point?" Jeff asked.

"Who knows?" I said.

"Jesus Christ," Carl said. "Here we go again."

"Yeah," Dwayne said. Clarence stood there looming over even Gordon and Overland by about six inches.

"Damn, he's big," Clint Jahn said to me.

"And he has, I'm told, about a 4.4 forty," I told him.

Ham looked at his people. "I'm sorry we are here again," he said. "I'm glad you are all with me."

Mariano looked at Sebastian. "We will have back up in four, ESU in ten."

"Can't wait," Mariano said. "There's a kid in there."

There was a large double door in the middle of the wall in the back of the room. Ham spoke to Clarence in a whisper as we moved as quickly and quietly as we could. There were a few lamps—Coleman lanterns like I thought. The place was remarkably clean. They had probably been coming there a long time. I'd bet Foster had paid off the college security people. Clarence looked down and smiled at Ham.

"Guys, it worked once before. Clarence can get through the door."

I looked at the Giant and in his face I knew. If there was a child on the other side of that door, he was going in. Dwayne looked at it and whispered, "Clarence, hit the right door, I'll hit the left." Clarence nodded.

"What am I, chopped liver?" Carl asked.

"You're a step too slow with them knees," Dwayne said with a smile. "This is ten years and two operations later."

Carl nodded. Clint walked over and the Chief spoke. "Okay, let's get four guns behind them. Vivian, Gordon, myself, and Creed. Then Overland and Carl. If Dwayne or Clarence have any problem after getting through, make sure they are okay. The rest of the cops after, and everyone else after that have an eye out. If something happens to the people in front of you, stop. If we had a week we couldn't plan this like we should, so we are winging it."

We all positioned ourselves. Clarence and Dwayne got ready. You could feel the tension. Then Dwayne held up his hand. He walked over to the large double door and tried the handle. It opened slightly inward. He looked through a crack less than an inch wide he'd made. I shook my head. The guy that went outside would have gone back in, we should have known. Mariano ran over and looked.

The chanting was louder with the door open a crack. There were not quite twenty of us. Mariano looked in the crack and turned. "About twenty, all facing an altar and Foster behind it. There are doors in the back, and he's close to it. Someone get that son of a bitch."

Gordon moved next to him. Dwayne and Clarence as well. Ham and I were right behind them. Everyone else behind us, and then Clint Jahn appeared at my right.

"Ready?" Mariano asked. Everyone nodded. "Keep quiet until they see us."

He pushed the doors open into the room, which was fairly well let. Clean like the front room had been. There was a little girl asleep in the corner; we'd made it with time to spare. Foster would have been looking at us but he had turned his back for something. All of his people were looking forward, chanting something. They were in four rows of five, and one person stood in front. We were within feet of them when Foster turned.

"Move!" Gordon bellowed.

Ham, Clint, and I all ran for Foster. I have to hand it to him. He saw us and without expression turned and ran toward one of the four doorways in back of the room. I heard both Vivian and Manfre yell, "Drop them!" and then gunshots. More of the cops fired. As we closed on the doorway Foster went through, the way was barred by the man that had stood alone in the front of the group.

"Get out of the way, Manny, or I'll kill you," Ham called to him.

I raised the Kimber 45 toward him, hoping Mariano and Gordon had been right. Before I got it all the way up, Clint Jahn crashed into him and the hook was an inch or so in Manny's neck.

"If you move, I will tear your throat out," Jahn told him and Manny froze. Whatever he believed was waiting for him in the afterlife, he didn't want to get there via Clint's hook.

Ham went through the door first. I threw a quick look around. Clint Overland had picked up the child and cradled her and was moving toward the way we came in. One of the cult members made to move on him, but Terry got to him first. Terry must have cut him fifteen times before he fell. Mariano's cops were cuffing some of the freaks.

"Chief!" I yelled as loud as I could. I pointed at the doorway. Foster went that way. I took off, not waiting to see who might follow. There were stairs going up. It was much darker and I could barely make out Ham. I took the stairs two at a time. At the top, there was another huge room. There was a set of circular iron stairs that led up to a landing about twenty-five feet higher with a cathedral ceiling. High windows to the far left and right admitted dim moonlight, and there were more lamps here and there. Foster stood on the top of the landing. It wasn't as big as the room below it, but it was the size of a large commercial space. Behind him were four doorways that seemed to be the theme of the building. There were chairs arranged to face the landing. They had used this room.

"Well, here we are, Ham." Foster's voice came through speakers to our left and right.

"The bastard has a sound system here. Probably used it to address the troops," I said.

At the top of the circular stairs was a new steel door. I realized Foster had planned for this. If he got that door closed, I'd bet there was a way out of at least one of the four doorways. There was also an archway that seemed to be boarded up to the right of the last door.

Foster stood on the landing and the iron door was open. The doors in the back were open. I was certain one or both would lead to a way out, and everything that I knew about Foster told me if he went through those doors he'd disappear.

He stared down at us. He swept his hand toward the rusting iron stairs.

"I'm waiting, brother." Foster's voice echoed off the walls. I heard water dripping somewhere.

My gun was out, at my side. Ham's eyes were locked on Foster and Foster's eyes were locked on him. From the bits of noise I was hearing, I was able to decipher our people were moving closer to us. There were a few gun shots. I heard Mariano's voice call out in the distance, "Drop your weapon and lie on the floor hands behind your head NOW! I won't tell you again!" There were three shots. I guess the guy didn't comply.

"Jimmy, I have to do this," Ham said to me.

"Ham, if he gets past you he's gone. Your family is at risk."

"He won't."

"If he gets past you, more kids die. More kids are tortured the way you were. I know you have to end this, but stopping him, making sure we stop this cycle of monsters being made, that's what's important. Making sure your family is safe," I whispered harshly at him and shook his shoulder. "If he gets past you, your family will never be safe. *Never*."

"He won't get past me." I had never heard anyone say anything with such certainty. I heard footsteps, a lot of them, getting closer. I was tempted to let Ham go. Even with everything at stake, I had never heard such conviction. He needed to do this. But I couldn't risk it. I also knew that once I went through that door I'd empty the .45 into Foster.

"You're not armed. He's a killer, Ham. You hired me. I'm doing this."

"I'm sorry, Jimmy," Ham said to me, sadness in his voice. The head-butt he gave me rocked my head back, and he chopped down on my carotid artery. I dropped like a stone. My gun fell and ended up a few feet away from me. I was trying to move as Ham went to the stairs. I managed not to lose control of my bladder or throw up, but that took effort.

"Take my gun, you fool!" I managed to get out. My voice was thick and slurred, and my face felt like it was on fire and everything was blurry. But I heard rather than saw him going up the iron staircase. I tried to get up, and heard the huge steel door slam shut and the bar behind it thrown into place. A battering ram wouldn't make it through that goddamned door. Why did he close the fucking door?

You'd have an easier time taking a sledge to a stone wall than trying to break that door down with the bar in place.

"You goddamned fool," I said softly, knowing that if I were in his place I might have gone up there, too. Except I'd have emptied my gun into him. I tried to get up and fell. Foster and Ham faced each other. I rubbed my eyes. The footsteps and voices got louder, and a few seconds later Mariano stood next me as he and Clarence helped me up. Clarence steadied me. The lights dimmed and Foster was a silhouette now.

"What have we got, Jimmy?" Mariano asked.

I shook my head. Clarence, Dwayne, and Carl were there now. Then Jeff. I almost fell over and Clarence steadied me again.

We watched. Foster and Ham closed the gap between them. They circled each other, their eyes locked. I leaned on Clarence, getting my bearings back. Mariano stared.

"I swear to God, if Ham wasn't so close to him I'd kill Foster," Mariano said.

I nodded. "My thoughts exactly." I pointed toward the landing. "Those doors, in the back there are passageways. That wood over there with a few broken planks. I have no idea what is behind it. Foster's had years to plan. If he makes it past Ham, he's gone. Guaranteed."

"Okay." Mariano turned and looked at Carl, Dwayne, and Clarence. "The brute squad is hereby deputized. Break that fucking door down."

"Weren't we deputized earlier?" Carl asked.

"Not for manual labor," Mariano said.

"It's beyond even them. Chief, he learns from

mistakes—both his and others. Getting in was easy, but after what happened in Manhattan, he has a barrier between us and him. He wanted Ham up there. He makes contingencies, and contingencies for the contingencies. It's not just an old iron door, it's steel and there are bars behind the door."

"Who closed it?"

"I don't know. I was on the floor trying not to black out."

The Big 3 looked at each other and then they looked at the door. Clarence took a deep breath and looked at the other two. They nodded.

"Beyond even us?" Clarence asked. "We'll see about that," his low voice rumbled. Carl bent over, picked up my gun, and handed it to me. That was probably the longest he'd talked since I'd met him.

"You may want this," he said with a smile. I grumbled.

"Let's do it," Dwayne said as he went for the stairs. Clarence and Carl followed.

Mariano and I watched as they circled each other. My whole body tensed and I shook off the last of the dizziness. I knew he had to do this. I thought about his wife and children. How could I tell them if Foster killed him? I couldn't, I answered myself. Ham will win. Jeff made his way over. The echo of people yelling made its way to where we were as the cops came through other parts of the building. Ham might have figured a lot of this out as well. He was going to face his demons now. He'd try to save his brother, but he was done having the past loom over him.

Mariano looked at me for a moment and turned his

attention back to the combatants above us. "Nice knot on your head there."

"Yeah," I said.

"Who did that?" he asked.

"My client," I said, a tad angry over it still.

"Hmmm. You may want to discuss that with him."

"I intend to," I said.

"Maybe we should have it put in the retainers," Jeff started. "That any injury inflicted on a principal of the company by the client results in the retainer being doubled."

I looked at him, gritted my teeth, and said, "Maybe."

Mariano snorted and Jeff smiled.

"How well do you guys shoot?"

"I'm good, Jimmy is fair. I'd say he was good but he's never used it thus far."

"If he gets past Ham, we turn him into Swiss cheese. I can justify it. I can't let that thing lose into the population. First timers usually miss out of uncertainty or nerves," Mariano said, looking at me briefly. "He gets one warning to lay down. If he doesn't, we open up."

"Chief, I don't claim to know the law as well as you but I don't think that's the law. You shoot a fleeing felon, you'll end up charged."

"Jimmy," he said softly, turning to me. "I won't have him killing more children."

"I'm pretty certain he has a gun in his waist band," Jeff said. "If he happens to point it at us I'll yell gun."

"Those reasons people might miss," I said, in a voice that sounded too cold to be coming from me, yet it did. "They won't be a factor."

Clarence was trying to force the door. The small

platform at the top of the iron stairs made it impossible for more than one of them to be on it at a time.

"Fucked to a fare thee well," I muttered, watching them.

Mariano nodded. "Not for lack of trying," Jeff said. Even from a distance a way we saw all of Clarence's massive muscles bunch and as he pushed on the door, looking to bend it, I figured.

Foster put the mike on the floor and the sound system was on. We could hear them talking. Foster wanted that, too.

More people had come up the stairs. When Foster's voice sounded, no one had to call out quiet; a hush fell over the chamber. Everyone looked at the platform. They were five feet apart. As they faced each other, they were both calm. Foster stood there, his hands clasped in front of him, and Ham's hands dangled loosely at his sides. Both of them had a slight bend in their knees, and despite the placid appearance the feeling of coiled energy exuded from them.

A groan came from between Clarence's teeth and he put everything he had on the door. I couldn't tell from this distance with the light if he'd made any progress. Dwayne switched with them. Carl would go last. He had performed record breaking feats of grip strength, I'd been told. The other two would put all they had into it and maybe he'd have something to work with.

"Your life, which you do not deserve, your wealth, your family, all of this...I gave you. Despite the fact you were put here to serve, you have these gifts. I even allowed you to keep my children."

"You relinquished any claim on those children. They were not your property, they were yours to raise with love and to teach them to be good. You disqualified yourself from being their parent."

"That is not why they were put here, either. They are here to serve higher powers. They were put here to serve them. There are things greater than us, which should be paid heed."

"You speak as if you had conviction, but you're just a freak that gets off on hurting kids. You manufactured a couple of victims. And there *is* something greater than all of us—our children."

Foster chuckled. "No, you're right in that almost all of these so called apostles are gratified when they hurt children. And they are loved for that. The pain they cause feeds them. It feeds me. But not I. I believe in, and I have seen...I carry their power."

"Is that why you make the kiddie porn?"

"Money is required in this realm. I have made a lot of it. You have a choice to make now. Once you have, I will disappear. I have the money to reemerge in any one of a dozen places around the world with an identity that is already real."

"A choice?" Ham asked.

"You are my brother. I still looked out for you as best I could. Even our Master doesn't know what will happen to you, but you could be with us. Join me. Come with me. In time we will bring Sophia and the children to us and you can have them back. I give you this choice as opposed to just killing you."

There was silence. Ray Gordon had apparently made it into the room. How a guy six five can get that goddamned close without me knowing is beyond me.

"Chief, deputize the SEAL."

"Deputize for?" Gordon asked softly, also watching Ham and Foster.

"You're deputized," Mariano said.

"If Foster gets past Ham, those doorways in the back of the platform lead to God knows where. We shoot Foster. We can't let him get away," Jeff said. I hadn't noticed but his gun was in hand.

"I can hit him from here," Ray said. "And not hit Ham."

"It's a long shot," I said.

"Not for a SEAL," Jeff said.

"That would be the wise decision," Mariano said. He turned to look at me. "You're neck deep in this, Jimmy. Any input?"

I took a deep breath. "Yeah. Ham hired me to find this creature. But there's more to it. He's a child of the secret. I don't rank abuse, but I think even Vachss would say his is one of the worst cases he's ever heard of or seen. He has a chance to correct it. No, not correct it. Nothing will make it go away. He has a chance to take the power over what was done to him away. Give it to him."

"He's SBS," Gordon said. "They can give us a run for the money."

"Meaning?" Mariano asked.

"He's a killing machine. Ham is strong, very fast, and almost superhuman. He knows what he is doing. He's as good with his hands as anyone. But he is up against someone that has likely killed dozens. Foster knows a hundred different ways to kill a man without searching his memory. Foster is up to something. He wants to bring Ham back into the fold. Ham," I paused. "Ham wants to try to save his brother."

Ray nodded.

"And you say give him a chance, Jimmy? It's a chance Foster could get away."

"He's right, Jimmy," Ray said.

"I know. Ray," I said, turning to my friend. "Despite everything you've been through in your life, you believe in God, you're religious. Right?"

"Yes."

"We don't have the time for me to tell you, but for everything to have happened in the way that it happened, to bring us here, to bring Ham there," I nodded my head toward the platform, "I think Ham is being given his chance."

"What if he loses?" Jeff asked.

"Win or lose is up to him. But he has been given the chance. That's what I believe, right here right now at this moment. Maybe I will see it different. There is something else, too. Ham is fighting for his family now. That will be a big factor. I say, no. I plead, give him his chance."

"It could also be his chance to die," Ray said softly, not with sarcasm but with honesty.

"I know that," I said. "More importantly, he knows that."

We all looked at Mariano. "Then he has his chance," he said after a moment.

Carl groaned with monumental effort. Although it was a distance away, and it was dark, I could see he barely managed to bend the top corner of the door about an inch. He near collapsed from the effort. They'd not make it in time.

Everyone in the room watching and listening—if you talked to them after, it seemed everyone saw something different while we all looked at the same thing.

Gordon leaned over and looked at me. "Nice bump there," he said.

"He got it from his client," Mariano said. "In the future he will ask them not to do that and charge them extra if they do," he said.

"I'm going to put that in the retainer," Jeff said.

"Good ideas," Gordon said, looking at the two adversaries on the platform.

"You people are a fuckin' riot," I said.

"No extra charge for the humor," Ray said.

"That's good," Jeff said. "We can't afford it."

"Because you waste all our money on prunes and bran," I said.

"Regularity is important," Mariano said.

Ham spoke again. "*I* will give *you* a choice.

"You are my brother. You were tortured as I was. The difference is I had a family, a family that loved me, that protected me. I was rescued. They helped me. You never had that chance. No one ever loved you. You became a monster, like the monsters that gave birth to us. Stop this now. Come with me. We will get you a lawyer, the best. You have money, I have money. They'd give you a deal, and you can give up hundreds of freaks. You can get help. You can make up for what you did. I will be there for you. Let's go. After what was done to you, people will understand. You can still have a life. Sophia, me, the kids, we will all be there for you. You will have to make up for what you have done but you can still have a life. You don't have to be what they tried to make you."

When Foster didn't reply Ham kept talking. "When

we were children, you looked out for me then, too. You'd bring me food and didn't let them see. You gave me a blanket once. If you hadn't been taken away, if you had been with someone that gave you love, you'd have turned out differently. You have a chance to change that now. Change it, brother. Let me help you, Billy. You don't have to be what they tried to make you."

There was a gap between Ham's offer and Foster's reply, maybe a second. As long as it took for a smile to form.

"What makes you think I don't like who I am?" He shook his head.

If I had heard Hitler recite excerpts from *Mein Kampf*, I doubt it would have sounded as cold and as evil as that reply.

Ham was silent as Foster continued. "I was born to do what I do. I am here to make a difference. You aren't foolish enough to believe in God? A God who allows children to be raped as you were? My sexual preferences are not along those lines but what kind of God would allow that at all? Children mean nothing to me. They were put here to help me. The true power to be. You don't punish a lion for killing an elk. It does it because it needs to, it is its nature. If you want to cherish children, do so. If you want to rape them, do so. None of that matters to me. The political climate of this country is perfect now. Elevate perpetrators over victims, sheep pitying the wolves.

"I am touched, Ham. In your childish way, you mean what you say. I would prefer you come with me, that I don't have to kill or maim you. Come with me. That is the only choice here. Return to your destiny or die. I am not expecting you to make that choice, but I am still giving you the chance. All of this...I did everything to bring you back to us. To me. To the Master. Fulfill your destiny, brother. The door will yield to the strength of our comrades in time. Or Chief Mariano's Emergency Service Unit will get through. You need to decide now. Come into the fold or I take what I have given you and your life. I wish for you to be with me."

"Foster," Ham said coldly. "That's what you want me to call you. Billy is dead." He nodded to himself. "I have searched for you for years. You were abused just as I was. But the choices you make now are irredeemable. As an adult you knowingly hurt children. You are cruel and murderous. For years I agonized over what happened to you. You should not have threatened my family. You will not leave here alive."

"Easier said than done, brother. You killed one man in adrenaline fueled rage. I have killed dozens. Men, women, children. Life means nothing to me. Even yours. While you looked for me I was right there." I went cold now as he withdrew a long double edged knife.

"Ah shit," Gordon said. "Our chances just got much worse."

He knew what he was doing. He let Ham see the knife because Ham knew what he could do with it. When a pro shows you his knife, it was because of the effect it would have. Foster knew what Ham was capable of. I knew that Ham knew what Foster could do and that he planned something. He had to. The real question was, could he follow through and kill his brother? To have even a small chance against a knife, you had to be committed to the killing of your opponent. Television was where you kicked it out of his hands, the music swells, and the good guy prevails. A knife in the hands of an amateur was hard to overcome. Being barehanded against a pro, well, you didn't have much of a chance.

I had spent more than thirty-eight of my forty-seven years learning to fight. I knew violence. I was when I needed to be, violent. Knives were an up close and personal equalizer. Hand-to-hand, Ham had some edges. His strength and his speed and his training. Foster could probably stab him or slash him a half dozen times even if he caught him on a fully committed rush. Ham knew about this stuff and he knew how smart Foster was and how deadly. I prayed, actually prayed, which I do not do often, that Ham was as smart as I thought he was. Clarence started working the bend in the door and Dwayne appeared to be holding Carl from falling off the stairs due to the enormous effort he'd made.

Ham suddenly rushed forward, his left hand up high and turned palm facing inward. His body angled, cutting down on the target he presented, and the arm held so a slash wouldn't hit a major vein or artery. Not much help against a stab, and Foster would know that. Foster danced away, not backward but circling to his left. His arm moved like a snake. They ended up apart but Ham had been stabbed or cut at least five times. A few more clashes like that, and Foster would bleed so much he just collapsed.

"Clarence, we got to get in there!" someone shouted.

As these thoughts went through my mind, I also stared in wonder for lack of a better word. I swear, it could have been a trick of the light but standing here now, long after it happened I'd say no. There were two flashes at the same time. Like old fashioned camera flashbulbs going off. A white light around Ham and around Foster. It was much harder to describe. If light could flash black, I'd say that. Rethinking it, it was a flash but it was like Foster was drawing the light into him, like a black hole would. The more I think about it, it was an impression of light rather than seeing the light. Or was it?

"Did I see that?" I said aloud without realizing it.

"The light?" Mariano asked. "And the unlight?"

"You saw it, too?" I asked him.

He didn't answer. Later, Ray and Jeff would say they were aware of something but couldn't say what it was. Jeff said it was probably a trick of the light. Ray never said anything but I heard him very softly say, "Come on, Ham."

I saw absolutely nothing Ham could use as a weapon. Foster feinted twice. The first didn't work, but the second did. His arm moved again and he tagged Ham maybe three more times. This time, though, Ham clubbed him with a sloppy off balance right hand that still knocked him back a good distance. Ham used that opportunity to take his belt off. Ham's left hand hung a little lower and he'd almost certainly been cut on that arm.

"If you had a gun, you'd have won," Foster said as he whirled the knife around, with the handle in his palm and the blade hidden by his forearm.

For a good person, a person with a good heart, to be able to kill his own brother when it became necessary would be harder than anything I could think of at the moment. I don't think I could.

Ham's left hand dropped a little lower; he was weakening from the wounds. Foster feinted again, and again got in, made his cuts, and got out. Ham swung the belt hard but it went very wide. His lead hand dropped lower, and he sagged a little. I suddenly became aware of Sophia standing next to me. She cried silently but said nothing. If I found out who let her in, I'd kill them.

Even at this distance I could feel the sadness coming from Ham. Sophia had told me he would still cry sometimes, when they spoke of his brother. How he wished he could find him. Help him. He prayed, actually prayed that his brother was ok. I'd made a terrible mistake. I should have urged Mariano that we shoot. Ham would die, the family would be broken, and it would be on me. Strong as he was, it had been too much for him. Sophia buried her face in my shoulder and wept.

Ham's left hand dropped further still, he sagged more, and Foster got his opening. With his speed he'd take Ham with a stab in the neck. Then he'd twist and work the knife back and forth. I wish I didn't have to watch.

Like lightning Foster was in, almost too fast to see. I didn't see Ham get the hand up, and Foster's knife plunged in to Ham's arm, not his neck. Ham had dropped the belt and swung hard with his right arm as he twisted and he landed on the side of Foster's head. I heard the sound. He knocked Foster half way across the platform, and as Ham turned violently I saw the knife was still in his arm. He cried out in pain, drew his arm in, but straightened almost immediately, the cry transformed into a roar. I'd heard that sound before. I'd made it. Primal rage and power. I had the impression of the white light again as Ham rushed forward into Foster, who was off balance and staggering, trying to recover. The light and the unlight clashed again as Ham kept moving forward full speed then the unlight disappeared. I could swear the light was emanating from the pocket where Ham had put the stone Clint Jahn gave him. The boards covering the arch-shaped hole in the wall broke instantly under the force, and Foster went through, emitting a roar of his own. The rage that came from him was rage at losing. The momentum carried him and Ham spread his arms wide, the knife still through the left one, and he slapped both hands into the stone on either side. I'd heard Foster for about two and a half seconds. It faded as he fell but almost immediately, it began to echo. To say it was eerie because it stopped suddenly but the echo continued over and over, was an understatement.

Clarence yelled and the door bent. Carl grabbed it as they somehow managed to squeeze their huge frames together and they both pulled. Dwayne, having no room to work on the door, had grabbed their belts in each hand and pulled them back. It was them or the door and the door gave. The bar snapped and the door opened. If Dwayne had kept pulling all three of them would have gone over the edge of the stairs but as the bar snapped, he switched up and was pushing on them. When we got up there we saw those boards prevented access to shaft that might have been a well at one time.

Ham had collapsed and was on his knees when Sophia ran to him. Mike, Ray, and I were close behind. Mike and Ray went to the arch and I stopped briefly with Sophia. His good arm held her and he was taking deep, controlled breaths. I joined Mike and Ray. I was wondering if Foster was alive how I might be able to finish him off with witnesses around; it disturbed me that I wasn't disturbed by that thought. We knew from the sound Foster had fallen. The Chief's flashlight revealed a shaft or maybe a well. There were rungs on the wall, but they were not uniform, and some had been broken. There were a few large holes in the walls and cloudy water in the bottom. It did not smell brackish, which I wondered about. It rippled like when you throw a stone into a pond. Rocks protruded from the water in places. The sound emanating from Foster lasted about two and a half seconds. The water was about seventy feet down. That appeared to match up considering there would have been momentum propelling him forward before he fell. That water was not something you would want to go for a swim in; forget about falling seventy feet or so into it.

EMTs arrived and were tending to Ham. There were a lot more people and later on almost everyone I talked to had a different impression of what they saw. Vivian had come in and saw most of it and whatever she saw, she kept to herself. The EMTs decided to leave the knife in Ham's arm until they got to the hospital and bound up his other wounds. He had a number of stabs and slashes on his arm and upper torso. Although none were too bad they were bleeding a lot if you looked at the blood from each wound as a part of a whole.

In the end, Ham had extensive damage to that arm and had surgery ahead of him. The pinky and ring finger of his left hand wouldn't move. Other than that, the wounds were stitched and he was given meds and a tetanus booster shot.

The doctor treating him suggested staying overnight to be cautious and his response was, "Not with my insurance. It's what New York State chose for me. I'm self-employed." The doctor nodded sadly. "According to the MRI and the X rays, you will need surgery or your pinky and ring finger won't function properly. You really should consider staying."

"I can't," Ham said. "Besides, Doc, being home with my wife and kids will heal me up much faster than being anywhere else."

Of the cultists, only seven survived. None of them talked. The initial indication of the freaks at the hotel was as we thought, poison, but we would never know for sure if they knew what they were drinking. I know what I saw. I know what I felt. I would see Ham a few days later. His kids were home. Doc and Smitty and their family had Sam back. He seemed to be dealing with it okay. I had a nice bruise on my forehead. Considering the last two major outings I had which ended up with me shot and beaten to a pulp, I'd take it. You know, insurance investigators don't normally have these things happen to them. I needed to look for more trial prep.

Foster was more than just well off. The man that had taken him had been very wealthy. No one knew where he was or if he was still alive. He had been worth in the hundreds of millions and Foster was his only heir. He had probably used the idea of Satanism as a way to build and control followers. From what I've read and learned from Clint, Satanism was a Christian construct. The so-called true believers believed in a variety of entities and Satan wasn't one of them. The idea of devil worshippers had been conjured up by the Church. And of course there were other people that said different. Foster had said things that indicated he had committed himself to something. But he also used Hollywood imagery to control people like the man that had controlled his biological father. In the end, they were evil. They were monsters but they were also just freaks that hurt children.

The little girl had been drugged but she was okay and she was with her family now. I went to see Ham a few days after he got out of the hospital.

Ham grimaced when he saw my forehead. "I am sorry, Jimmy."

I smiled. "I know. I know that you had to face him and try to save him. If I had a chance to fight my demons, I would. But I owe you for the head-butt and I am billing you extra."

He coughed and laughed. "Fair enough. If my arm heals well enough we can do some training together and I'll give you the chance to even up. Send the bill, and make sure you make some money after your expenses. Apparently, as I was his brother, I am entitled to Foster's estate. I'll make sure that anyone he hurt is taken care of. And their families. It's not a small amount."

"Good by me, Ham." I hesitated. "I need to ask you something."

"You can ask me anything. You helped save my family and no amount of money will ever pay that debt. You figured him out."

"Mariano did, too. You might have also but you were too close. He was a master at manipulation."

He nodded.

"Then I will ask you something and ask you for something."

"Do so," he said softly.

I told him what I saw. What some of the others saw, the light and the anti-light. On reflection it seemed better than un-light. I asked him if he saw it or was aware of it. He reflected for a while.

"I'm not aware of it. But far be it from me to say what happened. I felt power in me, even after he cut me. I am not a religious person, Jimmy. I agree with Vachss. If there is a God, he should be sued for malpractice. I get free will, but not harm against children. I do believe in my way. I pray sometimes. I talk to him more often. I can't tell you if what I saw when I was upstate was the creature that was my biological parent, or if I imagined it due to the trauma. Some of it was so horrible, only Vachss and I know about the full extent. There are things I have not even told my wife, because of the pain she feels about it. So in the end, I don't know."

I nodded. I still do not know exactly what I saw and who am I to say it had to be a trick of the light?

"Finish your book, Ham. You are what Vachss describes as a transcender. People should know those things."

"I very well may do that. It does help as well."

"I know you will always protect children. We need people that have that principle dominate." He nodded. "Are you at peace with what happened to Foster?"

"I did everything I could." He took a deep breath. "What I said was true. Although we were both abused, I had my parents who loved me and taught me empathy and kindness. He was indoctrinated, and his abuse continued. But he knew right from wrong and as an adult he chose to continue his path."

I was meeting Rhea so I got up to leave. I left him with his final words on the subject ringing in my ears. "I grieve for him as a child. He had a choice and he made it. He threatened my family. I do not regret what I did to the man, and I carry no guilt over it."

I shook his hand and gently put my hand on his left shoulder. I was almost through the door when my phone rang. It was Mariano.

"Hey, Chief," I answered.

"Hey, Jimmy, are you with Ham by any chance?"

"I am, Chief."

"Jimmy can you put me on speaker?"

"You're on speaker, Chief," I said. "It's just Ham and I."

"We haven't been able to recover Foster's body."

AFTERWORD

I hope you enjoyed this book, my friends. When I write, I do the best I can to make it real. Truth through fiction. That was the method that Andrew Vachss used, and I follow that formula to the best of my ability. Although no one does it as well as he did.

On the surface, Creed vs Satanists may not seem real. The truth of the matter is occult and satanic crimes are rare. While they do happen, when they happen most often you will find freaks that enjoy hurting children making a half-assed culture or religious defense to justify their actions. There are exceptions—as with everything. The abuse portrayed in this book has happened, is happening, and will happen again. I base all of the examples of abuse I write about on actual cases with the permission of the person who went through it. They will obviously always be anonymous. But if you think that these instances are far-fetched—keeping a child in an iron cage under the stairs, for example—you aren't familiar with what happens all too often.

Andrew and I spoke frequently, averaging what I assume was about an hour a week for almost seven years. One day we discussed what I presented to you in this book. Why is it that some kids endure horrific abuse and end up transcenders—people who dedicate their lives to protecting children and others from becoming monsters?

If we could figure out that formula, he told me, we would have a huge piece of the puzzle solved. I suggested to him that, in some or even several cases, after having endured abuse, there was someone now in those children's lives giving them love and affection, teaching them empathy. "That idea, John, does have promise," he said.

Ham had that love, and Foster did not.

If you enjoyed the story, I did a good job. If I entertained you and made you angry, I did a good job. If you read this story and made understand more about what is going on all around us, every day, then I did a good job. If I gave you a glimpse into a world that exists next to yours—but you didn't really know it—I did a good job.

If you liked it, please spread the word. As the man himself often said, word of mouth is any writer's greatest treasure.

IF YOU LIKE THIS, YOU MAY ALSO ENJOY: WICHITA PAYBACK

WICHITA DETECTIVE BOOK ONE BY PATRICK ANDREWS

1940s Wichita, Kansas

Dwayne Wheeler, a slightly felonious private detective, plies his trade in the city's sub-culture of bookmakers, bootleggers and hookers. When he is hired to solve the murder of a local bookie and dear friend, the case is quickly linked to the arrival of a Kansas City mobster on the scene.

Sensing a takeover of local bookmaking and criminal activity in the works, Dwayne's investigation leads him into the upper echelons of Wichita society and into the arms of corrupt police. And it isn't long before some very powerful people decide it would be advantageous if he turned up face down in the Arkansas River.

Will Dwayne be able to use all his highly developed skills of self-protection to stay alive as he gathers the evidence he desperately needs to solve a murder and prevent K.C. gangsters from invading his beloved city?

Wichita Payback is book one in a historical private eye series that follows Dwayne Wheeler—a tough and hardboiled detective.

AVAILABLE NOW

ABOUT THE AUTHOR

You know that guy you picture when you read an old time PI novel? The one who stows a bottle of halfway decent whiskey in his bottom desk drawer? The one who sports a constant five o'clock shadow and—on occasion—abrasions on his face and knuckles that makes you wonder what the other guy looks like? Who has dark circles under his eyes because he hasn't slept more than a couple of hours since he pulled that impossible-to-solve case? He takes his work seriously but never himself? Well, that guy exists in the persona of John A. Curley–a martial arts trained, veteran Private Investigator, who is adept at tech and has a way with words, even if he does hunt and peck on the keyboard.

In his 35-year-career, Curley has worked locally, nationally and globally on wrongful death cases, divorce and custody cases, missing person cases, personal protection assignments and high-profile election fraud cases. He has logged thousands of hours on over 70 homicide cases—often with the defense relying heavily on the results of his investigations. Curley is perhaps the only investigator to warn his clients about Martin Frankel prior to his record setting fraud. He has currently assembled one of the most skilled and exceptional investigative team in the country.

His passion for child protection led him to his friend and mentor, the sadly deceased Andrew Vachss—the foremost authority on Child Protection the world has known. He adopted Vachss' principles and advocates for our most vulnerable population. He has been responsible for helping to remove children from abusive situations while ensuring that adult predators are put away. He also advocates for stronger laws against child predators.

Curley is a consummate storyteller whose bold, real-life experiences provide a perfect basis for intriguing dynamic fiction. His writing reflects the stunning need for change in how the legal system approaches child protection and domestic violence. His short stories have graced several periodicals and in the collection, *Protectors 2: Heroes.*

He is currently writing the Jonathan Creed PI series. *Bonds* is the first installment—with two sequels coming soon. He is also lending his considerable skill on the collaborative novel, *Hard Stop.* Joining Curley's characters are the literary creations of Wayne D. Dundee, S. A. Bailey and Michael Black. The proceeds of this team effort go to the Legislative Drafting Institute for Child Protection in memory of Andrew Vachss.